CHRISTMAS IN MY HEART

7

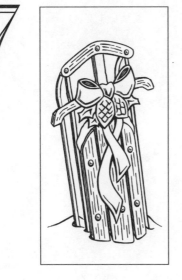

JOE L. WHEELER

REVIEW AND HERALD® PUBLISHING ASSOCIATION
HAGERSTOWN, MD 21740

This book was
Edited by Jeannette R. Johnson
Designed by Patricia S. Wegh
Cover illustration by Superstock/Currier & Ives, sled by Michael Biegel
Woodcut illustrations are from the library of Joe L. Wheeler
Typeset: 11/12 Goudy

PRINTED IN U.S.A.

02 01 00 99 98   5 4 3 2 1

R&H Cataloging Service
Wheeler, Joe L., 1936-   comp.
    Christmas in my heart. Book 7.

    1. Christmas stories, American.   I. Title:
Christmas in my heart. Book 7.

ISBN 0-8280-1388-8

Dedication

SUSAN P. HARVEY

Without her artistic and marketing genius, this series
might well have died an untimely death. Not only
that, but her encouragement, counsel, and enthusiasm
have meant everything to me.

Wherever this series may go, much of the credit
belongs to her, my long-time confidant and friend.

Books by Joe L. Wheeler

Christmas in My Heart, books 1-7
Christmas in My Heart, audio books 1-6
Dad in My Heart
Mom in My Heart
Great Stories Remembered
Great Stories Remembered, audio book
Old-time Christmas Stories
View at Your Own Risk

To order call, **1-800-765-6955**

Visit us at www.rhpa.org for more information on Review and Herald products.

Acknowledgments

"The Not-so-lowly Woodcut" (Introduction), by Joseph Leininger Wheeler. Copyright 1998. Printed by permission of the author.

"Red Shoes," by Anita L. Fordyce. Copyright 1983. Printed by permission of the author.

"Feliz Navidad!" by Carolyn Rathbun-Sutton. Copyright 1996. Printed by permission of the author.

"How Far Is It to Bethlehem?" by Elizabeth Orton Jones. Published in *The Horn Book Magazine*, December 1954, and as a book (Boston: The Horn Book, Inc., 1955). Reprinted by permission of The Horn Book, Inc., and the author.

"When Tad Remembered," by Minnie Leona Upton. Published in *The Youth's Instructor*, Dec. 22, 1925. Printed by permission of Review and Herald® Publishing Association.

"Snow for Christmas," by Virginia Everett Davidson. Copyright 1997. Printed by permission of the author.

"Anetka's Carol," by Eric Philbrook Kelly. Published in *St. Nicholas Magazine*, Dec. 1927.

"The First Crèche," by Arthur Gordon. Included in Gordon's anthology, *Through Many Windows*. 1983. Old Tappan, New Jersey: Fleming H. Revell Company. Reprinted by permission of the author.

"On Christmas Day in the Evening," by Grace S. Richmond. Included in *On Christmas Day in the Morning and Evening*, 1926. Copyright 1910 by The Ridgeway Company, New York: Doubleday, Page and Company.

"Kashara's Gift," by Lissa Halls Johnson. Copyright 1995 by Lissa Halls Johnson. Reprinted by permission of the author.

"Anniversary," author and original source unknown. If anyone can provide knowledge of the authorship, origin, and first publication source of this story, please relay this information to Joe L. Wheeler, in care of Review and Herald® Publishing Association.

"A Successful Calamity," by A. May Holaday. Published in *The Youth's Instructor*, Dec. 27, 1927. Reprinted by permission of Review and Herald® Publishing Association.

"The Carols of Bethlehem Center," by Frederick Hall. Included in *Stories Worth Re-reading*. Review and Herald Publishing Association, Washington, D.C., 1913. Text used by permission of Review and Herald® Publishing Association.

"The Red Envelope," by Nancy N. Rue. Published in *Focus on the Family Magazine*, December 1997. Reprinted by permission of the author.

"His Last Christmas," by Joseph Leininger Wheeler. Copyright 1998. Printed by permission of the author.

Contents

I Saw Three Ships

Old English Carol

I saw three ships come sailing in,
    On Christmas day, on Christmas day;
I saw three ships come sailing in,
    On Christmas day in the morning.

And what was in those ships all three,
    On Christmas day, on Christmas day;
And what was in those ships all three,
    On Christmas day in the morning?

The Virgin Mary and Christ were there,
    On Christmas day, on Christmas day;
The Virgin Mary and Christ were there,
    On Christmas day in the morning.

Pray, whither sailed those ships all three,
    On Christmas day, on Christmas day;
Pray, whither sailed those ships all three,
    On Christmas day in the morning?

O they sailed into Bethlehem,
    On Christmas day, on Christmas day;
O they sailed into Bethlehem,
    On Christmas day in the morning.

And all the bells on earth shall ring,
    On Christmas day, on Christmas day;
And all the bells on earth shall ring,
    On Christmas day in the morning.

And all the Angels in Heaven shall sing,
    On Christmas day, on Christmas day;
And all the Angels in Heaven shall sing,
    On Christmas day in the morning.

And all the souls on earth shall sing,
    On Christmas day, on Christmas day;
And all the souls on earth shall sing,
    On Christmas day in the morning.

Then let us all rejoice amain,
    On Christmas day, on Christmas day;
Then let us all rejoice amain,
    On Christmas day in the morning.

The Not-so-lowly Woodcut

Joseph Leininger Wheeler

Serendipitously, our first *Christmas in My Heart* anthology back in 1992 was illustrated with old-timey illustrations, most of them nineteenth-century woodcuts. That simple act locked me into that genre for the rest of my anthologizing career—or at least it *looks* that way. If you compare that very first collection with one of the more recent ones, most likely you will wonder about the wide disparity, quality-wise, between the illustrations. In that first collection we had no nineteenth-century illustration library to draw from, just a haphazard lot of Christmasy potpourri. And it shows. It shows most graphically when you try to match story line to illustration. It also shows in the poorer quality of image fidelity, for it is amazing how far our print-transfer technology has come in but six years! Back then, only the ultra-defined woodcut print reproduced well; halftones, lithographs, etc., weren't much of an option. But now almost any illustration is salvageable because computers can rescramble images with remarkable precision.

By the time the second collection came out, I had begun to build a nineteenth-century illustration library, though not enough to make much of a difference in the overall quality of print and fidelity to story line. But by the third collection the difference is almost glaringly obvious. The fourth was even better—and the fifth was the first collection I really felt good about: I was able to match the illustration to the story line in virtually every case.

Which brings me to one of the most frequently asked questions in my media interviews: "How do you choose your old-timey illustrations?"

Quite frankly, it ain't easy! For six years now, in my now several hundred book signings, I've had the opportunity to watch people as they approach these books. First of all, they are attracted to the Currier & Ives covers. Most of them have never seen Currier & Ives prints with that kind of brilliancy—they're used to rather dull flatness. The earliest generation prints had marvelous color and vitality, and Review and Herald editors have sought out the owner of the finest such reproductions in existence, bought the right to use them, printed them on state-of-the-art presses, then laminated them, in order to get the glow that delights so many thousands of browsers.

As for the inside illustrations, the introduction frontispiece is first to catch the eye. Because that is true, I spend a great deal of time searching for the most heart-tugging illustration I can find. Three seasons ago, I first incorporated a poem in that spot— No, I take that back! I stumbled on a wonderful old *St. Nicholas* woodcut of a little girl and a lamb, an illustration that implored just the right words to go with it. I knew, almost instantly, that only William Blake's "The Lamb" would do. Since then, I have inserted either a poem or a Christmas carol in that spot.

Moving further into the book, we come to the story illustrations. I'd guess the average reader takes these illustrations (mostly woodcuts) pretty much for granted, assuming that they came with the story. Nothing could be further from the truth! *Almost none of them came with the story.* Unlike magazines of today, not often did nineteenth-century magazine stories come illustrated; and if they did, most often a rather generic illustration was used just to break up the masses of print, but rarely did it tie in with the story line.

So I can almost hear you say, *where do you find them then?*

Let me tell you.

Nineteenth-century Magazines and Books

I don't know about you, but I *love* prowling around in antique and used-book stores. I lose all track of time (and often money, as well). During the past six years, in order to match illustration to story line, my wife, Connie, and I have invested an almost unbelievable amount of our time, energy, and income in seeking out these ever more-elusive and ever more-expensive pieces of Americana. *And,* I hasten to add, ever more-fragile and ever more-substandard, condition-wise. After all, when you're searching out old printed artifacts that are more than a century old, it's a near miracle to find any that are in top condition. If you are similarly addicted, you'll not be at all surprised by my next statement: *most nineteenth-century children's books are in poor condition. Moreover, most of their woodcut illustrations have significantly darkened and blurred, making them* very *difficult to reproduce.*

Old magazines come with other problems. First, the likelihood that you can find intact single issues of even a half-century-old magazine is becoming more and more unlikely. As many of you know, most of our anthologized stories come from a period I label "The golden age of Judeo-Christian story writing" (1870s to the 1950s). And that period, *especially* the years 1900 to 1940, has been under savage attack for almost 20 years now from antique dealers and buyers.

If you haunt antique or book malls or shows, I won't even have to explain. More and more dealers have ripped apart these wonderful old magazines in order to market framable prints, and even advertisements. Each time I see such a retail business, I sigh, knowing that the supply of intact period magazines has just shrunk some more! As a result of such wanton destruction of these scarce old magazines, surviving copies in good condition are going to become ever more difficult, if not impossible, to find at *any* price. And that loss is especially hard on us for it hits us with both barrels: old stories *and* old illustrations.

So what kind of illustrations do you find in these old magazines and books?

Well, first of all, there are some fascinating patterns that are now becoming clear to me after a lifetime of bookstore searching. The early books (up until mid-nineteenth century) rarely include many illustrations. In those days the supply of art work was limited, and the cost of incorporating such illustrations into the text was almost prohibitive. Until the 1880s, more often than not, what few illustrations there were (usually woodcuts or engravings) were bunched at the front of a given magazine issue. The rest of the issue (usually *at least* 75 per-

cent) would be a solid mass of unbroken type. Worse, most of the stories tended to be in the unillustrated part of the magazine. What this means is that we usually secure very few usable illustrations per dollar invested.

As we move into the gilded age (the 1880s), we see a remarkable change: illustrations become an integral part of family magazine printing. Remember that the golden age of woodcut illustration ebbed in the 1890s with the advent of lithography, the half-tone, and the photograph. Consequently, our available supply of woodcuts is now *at least* a century old. Also, keep in mind that non-rag paper tends to turn brown and crumble quickly. (Today's paperbacks are often printed on such poor paper that they start turning brown in months, rather than in decades, generations, or even centuries). Thus, as far as old books or magazines are concerned, you're always playing Russian roulette, paper quality-wise.

Now that we've set the stage, so to speak, let's get back to a question posed earlier: *How are the illustrations chosen?* Permit me, if you please, to walk you through the entire process.

Once the final batch of stories is agreed upon (usually distilled from at least three times that many), a schematic is made of each story—the number of people (and animals) featured, and the approximate age, sex, and characteristics of each one. The time period is noted, as is relative affluence and setting of action. Then comes the hardest part of all: finding *the* illustration for a given story. I'll confess to being a purist where these visual images are concerned. It always makes me angry when a text is misillustrated—and it's sad how often one is. (You wonder if the artist even bothered to read the text!) For each story I seek not just something that *could* be used, but something that so captures the essence of a character that, upon seeing it for the first time, I exclaim, "That's it!"

Once I sketch out all these schematics (including plot-lines), I begin another marathon. And, sadly, I have yet to find an easier way. Each day before beginning, I pray to the good Lord, entreating Him to sharpen my memory, as I flip through thousands of pages, that I will remember most of those variables so well that I won't lose the right ones by default. Each story has so many possible illustration tie-in hooks that this is an incredibly daunting task.

I pick out a stack of books (children's storybooks, travel books, old-time bound collections from periodicals such as *Harpers, Harpers Weekly, Harpers Young People, St. Nicholas, Youth's Companion, Youth's Instructor, Chatterbox, Cosmopolitan, Grahams, Scribners, Century, Girls' Own, Munsey's, Ladies' Home Journal, Ladies' Home Companion, McCalls, Delineator, The Strand, Wide Awake, Once a Week, Good Words, Golden Hours, Frank Leslie's Popular Monthly, Everybody's Magazine, Our Young Folks, Appleton's Juvenile Annual, Peter Parley's Annual, Appleton's Journal, Pall Mall Magazine, Cassell's Magazine,* and *National Magazine*) and I leaf through, one page at a time. When I find an illustration that is a possible match, I make a photocopy of that page and identify it so it can be refound, before returning that book to the shelves. All the while I search for *the* illustration for each story. Some days I may search for 12 to 18 hours straight without finding one really good one; other days I may find three or four. When I am all through, perhaps a month or so later, I choose the best illustration out of each batch, trying not to duplicate one that's been used in a previous collection. When I finally lock it up, blurry-eyed beyond belief, I can feel complimented should you matter of factly take the illustrations for granted, assuming they came with the stories. But it's worth it all when you tell me how very special a given illustration is to you! Needless to say, if we are to continue such a series of woodcut-illustrated collections long-term, it presupposes a continually-expanding illustration library, with an ever-longer searching period for *each book*.

So now, with this general introduction, we can safely move on to the subject of this introduction.

The Woodcut and Its Kindred

I had thought that last year's introduction, "From St. Nicholas to Santa Claus," was a tough one to research and write, but it was a breeze compared to this one. I've always loved art. In fact, I've taught art history, but that knowledge and expertise was totally inadequate to bring me through the introduction for this book. The problem has to do with the fact that the woodcut is merely one of a rather incestuous family of nineteenth-century types of illustration from which we draw. And they are anything but easy to understand or, worse, to tell apart. So I consulted book after book, trying to get a clear picture in my thick head. In the end, my perceived kitty cat of a task had grown into a tiger.

The following books constitute my reference base for this introduction: Douglas C. McMurtrie's *The Book: The Story of Printing and Bookmaking* (New York: Oxford University Press 1943); Herman Weschler's *Great Prints and Printmakers* (New York: Leon Amiel Publisher 1977); Gabor Peterdi's *Great Prints of the World* (London: Collier-Macmillan Limited 1969); Stephen Longstreet's *A Treasury of the World's Greatest Prints: From Dürer to Chagall* (New York: Simon & Schuster 1961); Kristian Sotriffer's *Printmaking: History and Technique* (London: Thames and Hudson 1966); Arthur M. Hind's *A History of Engraving & Etching* (Boston: Houghton Mifflin 1923); and Walter Shaw Sparrow's *A Book of British Etching* (London: John Lane the Bodley Head Limited 1926). However, for this section I am most deeply indebted to Weschler, Peterdi, and McMurtrie.

Nativity Woodcut by Albrecht Dürer

Before taking our little walk through graphic history, let's study the kindred types of illustration and note their similarities, as well as their differences. First of all, according to Gabor Peterdi, there are four general types of printed image reproduction:

Relief Process. Part of the printing block, or plate (wood, linoleum, plastic, metal, etc.), is etched away. Your uncut block is normally your printed surface. Relief printing does not lend itself to subtleties, but rather to boldness, more blank area than lines. What prints is only what is left after all else has been carved, or etched away. Hence, printing requires very little pressure.

Incised Process (lntaglio). The opposite of relief printing, the design is cut, scratched, or etched into the printing surface, or plate (copper, zinc, aluminum, magnesium, plastics, coated paper, etc.). Since the printed image emanates from the incisions (the sub-surface grooves), the printing necessitates tremendous pressure. It's actually a form of embossing.

Planographic Process (Lithography). Printing from a flat surface, often from a stone, makes for a faster process than the first two. Thus, it is conducive to spontaneous, direct, crayon, or brush drawing, as well as rich tonal variations and painterly color work.

Stencil Processes. In one of the oldest graphic methods known, ink is applied through cut-out sections of paper or other suitable material. It is particularly effective for flat or textured areas of printing, silk-screening being a form of it (Peterdi, 34-37).

Now that we understand these four general printing approaches, we can be more specific in terms of imaging methodology:

Woodcut. Next to stenciling, this is the oldest type of image reproduction, dating back to the seventh century A.D. in the Orient, and the fifteenth century in the West. The image is first drawn on a piece of smooth hardwood (early on, walnut or pear). Then the surface on both sides of a given line is cut away, leaving an image, or design, in relief, raised or isolated from the background. The surface is then smeared with ink and a piece of paper is pressed down on it to get print image. Very little pressure can be safely used, and there can be but a short life before wood block begins to crack or deteriorate. Good for bold contrasts and solid and textured areas.

Wood Engraving. Dates back to second half of eighteenth century. The English engraver, Thomas Bewick, unsatisfied with the range of the standard wood block design (limited as it was to the flow of the wood grain), sought out a harder wood (such as box elder) that could be cut across the grain without splitting or splintering. Using the same tools that goldsmiths used to engrave on metal it was possible to produce fine lines that could be brought closer together. These blocks tended to hold up longer than the old ones and could produce longer editions. Generally, the impression was given that white had been printed on a black background, whereas the earlier woodcuts appeared to be black on white.

Japanese Woodcut. In Japan woodcut printing early on achieved a sophistication and quality that made it an artistic benchmark. It was a product of a collaboration of professionals (artist-designer, wood-carver, and printer). The wood they used tended to be cherry.

Chiaroscuro Woodcut. This method (*chiaro* means

light; *oscuro* means dark) was first popularized in connection with Renaissance artists, such as Leonardo da Vinci. While Leonardo was able to juxtapose light and dark pigments for dramatic effect (study a copy of his "Mona Lisa" or "Ginevra di Benci"), other Renaissance masters used tinted paper, sketching their outlines with crayon or second color wash, then giving the impression of yet a third tone by adding touches of line white. It was a most complicated process for it necessitated the application of a succession of woodblocks, each inked to highlight additional colors. These wonderful hand-done images (no two exactly alike) are considered to be the first such colored prints in art history.

Metal Cut. Searching for even greater detail and longevity, artists and printers next turned to carving into copper, or some other soft metal. The methodology was similar to woodcutting—carving away, or lowering, the background to leave a printed surface in relief. The effect (white on black) was similar to that used by Bewick.

Intaglio Print. In Intaglio, the lines are cut, scratched, or bitten into the soft metal, such as copper, so that they lie *below the surface* of the material drawn on. When inked, the ink is naturally forced into these miniature furrows. Then when the surface ink is wiped clean, the imprisoned ink forms the design. To produce an Intaglio print, a piece of dampened paper is placed on the surface and run through a pressurized press, the porous paper drawing up the ink.

Following are a number of Intaglio approaches, all somewhat similar:

Line Engraving. The tools used for engraving, called *burins* or *gravers*, are uncomplicated. Each consists of a long, slim, metal shaft set within a wooden handle. When pushed through soft metal, they produce furrows much like a plough leaves in a loamy field. Since the objective is to secure clean lines, the metal that has been displaced is cleared away, and the rough edges are removed with a *scraper*, then burnished until smooth. Not surprisingly, the deeper the incision, the more ink the furrow will hold, and hence the darker and bolder the printed line.

Drypoint. Very similar to line engraving, a thin, pencil-sized tool that is either of fine steel or has a hard gem cutting edge (diamond, sapphire, or ruby), is used like a pencil. The artist scratches, or digs, into the surface. It too produces furrows but, unlike line engravings, the ragged, burr-like edges are not removed and provide a fuzzy but rich velvety line. Not surprisingly, such a surface is extremely fragile, and each print takes some of the plate with it. Consequently, editions are perforce small, and successful drypoint prints few. Furthermore, correcting drypoint errors is *very* difficult.

Etching. Instead of using metal tools, the artist uses acid as the cutting agent. The results tend to be truer as they can be systematically controlled and can result in a more fluid calligraphic type of drawing. First of all, the artist covers the printing surface with an acid-resisting wax-like substance called *ground*. After using lampblack to mute the shine, the artist sketches out the design with sharp, needle-like instruments. This etching needle cuts through the waxy ground to bare metal. After first protecting the edges and underside with a thick coat of varnish, the plate is immersed in an acid bath that bites into the exposed metal, leaving behind lines akin to engraving or drypoint. Should the artist wish to secure darker or heavier lines, the entire surface is recoated with acid-resisting ground (except for the lines to be darkened), then the plate is reimmersed in order to get a deeper bite.

Aquatint. The Latin term for acid, *aqua fortis*, is the base upon which this term is built. As with an etching, acid is used to create the image, but here a tonal look is sought in order to create more of a wash, or watercolor, effect. The secret here has to do with the fineness or coarseness of the acid-resisting resin coating the plate. When a deeper tone is desired, the acid is left on longer. This is a very difficult method to use and tends to produce uneven results.

Lift-ground Etching. As with aquatint, this is a tonal, rather than linear, approach. A most complex process, the texture results from the application of a solution made of sugar, liquid soap, and India ink. After it dries the entire plate is coated with a liquid ground. When *that* has dried, the plate is immersed in a bath of warm water that gradually seeps through the porous ground, and the sugar absorbing the water swells and "lifts" the ground from the image, leaving it exposed. Finally, an aquatint ground is laid in these lifted areas, and the plate is bitten in the conventional manner. A skilled print master, such as Picasso, who loved this method, would repeat this process a number of times to achieve more subtle tones.

Soft-ground Etching. This process came into being during the second half of the eighteenth century in order to simulate the look of crayon or pencil textures. The *soft-ground* (softer than regular ground) is laid evenly over the entire surface area. The plate is warmed in order to melt the resin enough to form a smooth surface; then the surface is covered with a piece of paper or fabric on which a drawing is made with a pencil, pen, or sharp instrument. This pressure causes resinous ground to stick to the paper or fabric so that when that is lifted off, the drawing is exposed on the metal. When immersed in acid, the result is an uneven broken line that appears to be drawn rather than incised. Renoir liked to use this method.

Mezzotint. Although rarely used in days gone by to create original prints, it is a very effective method of reproducing fine copies of old master paintings. The tools used (*rocker*, *roulette*, or other multi-pronged implements) have very sharp teeth, and when they are rocked back and forth on the surface, they so dig it up that it leaves a sea of dots. As a result, the artist starts with a rich monotonish velvety black surface, then uses *scrapers* to vary depth of the dots and, hence, determine how much ink each will hold. When he burnishes surface areas so they are smooth, and all the ink is wiped off, these portions will appear to be white. As a result, dramatic looking prints can be made. In recent years more artists are using this method to create original works.

Stipple Engraving and the Crayon Manner. Like mezzotints, this method is rarely used today. Initially used to make fine reproductions, it was supplanted by photography. It was created as a way of imitating crayon or charcoal drawings. First, the plate is covered with the usual etching ground, then a variety of tools with serrated edges (or the *chalk roll*) are worked over the surface. After the plate has been etched with acid, the artist touches it up with *gravers*. French printmakers have found this a very effective method for reproducing the Rococo drawings of Boucher, Fragonard, and Watteau.

Now let's turn to the planographic (or surface print):

Lithography. It was discovered around 1796 by Aloys Senefelder, a German author seeking a cheap way to print and publish his plays. He stumbled on this method by accident. Simply put, it is based on the antipathy of oil or grease for water.

To make a lithograph, the image is drawn with a greasy crayon or brushed with a greasy ink on the smooth-grained surface of limestone (or zinc or zincograph). The advantage of limestone or zinc is that they absorb water. Next, chemicals (gum arabic and nitric acid) are used to etch the unmarked areas of the stone or plate. After moistening the entire surface with a sponge, it will be seen that the lines and areas drawn or printed with greasy agents will repel the water, while the unmarked areas will absorb it. Then when a greasy ink is rolled over the entire surface, it will be accepted by the brushed or drawn areas, and repelled by the wet sections of unmarked stone or metal. Once inked, a piece of paper is placed over it and run through a press, transferring the image. A reproduction can be made by lithography that is so faithful it can be difficult to differentiate between an original and a copy.

Transfer Lithograph. Van Gogh rhapsodized about this magic transfer paper, for on it an artist could create out-of-doors, drawing directly with lithographic crayon that is then placed face down on a stone or plate and run through a press. The design is thus transferred to a printing surface and processed in the usual manner.

Whistler and Picasso also raved about this method because it permitted them to create designs far removed from their studios or printing presses.

Last of all, let's take a longer look at the stencil print. It was used in the Orient as far back as the Middle Ages, and in Europe, beginning with the Renaissance. Primarily, it was used as a vehicle for reproducing color and as a way of dressing up early black and white prints (earliest: Orient, as well as West use—playing cards and religious imagery). Later on, it was utilized extensively in creating posters and placards and, much later, for original prints. In its simplest form, apertures are cut of the desired shape in non-porous material—paper, plastic, or metal. Then when the stencil is attached to a blank surface and colored ink is rolled across, the image is reproduced. More elaborate effects can be achieved by imposing a series of stencils over the exposed area. After print dries, other stencils and colors can be applied, resulting in complex works of art. This *pochoir* process is frequently used to produce color reproductions and book illustrations.

Silk-screen Print (Serigraph). This method was not perfected until the twentieth century. It is based on the principle of stretching a strong fabric over a frame and forcing color through the fine mesh. The image is controlled by making part of the screen opaque, and part porous.

Monotype. Next to rubbing, this is about the simplest method of making a print there is. The plate can be almost any smooth surface, such as glass, metal, or porcelain. Heavy printing ink or oil pigment are best to use, with the artist painting directly on the smooth surface. To make an impression the artist places a sheet of paper on the plate, applies pressure, removes the paper—And voilá! A print! This simple type of print has been used by artists all down through the ages, from Michelangelo and Leonardo to Gaughin and Chagall.

(This section made possible by Weschler, 16-31; and Peterdi, 34-51.)

The Masters

I'll have to confess, where printmaking is concerned, at least, to being little better than an ignoramus. I had no idea that the supposedly lowly woodcut and its kin had such illustrious pedigrees. Worse, I have often put them down myself by saying, "What do I use? Oh, just old-timey woodcuts." How mistaken can a person be?

When was the first print made? Quite probably the first time someone rubbed a paper-like piece of material against a stone or wood form, turned it over and lo, a rubbing! Children still use this method to get reproductions from coins.

How far back do woodcuts date? According to Longstreet, at least back to 947 A.D.; according to Peterdi, back to 686 A.D. In China, according to Sotriffer, wooden stamping dates clear back to the ancient Egyptian and Babylonian civilizations. But the effective use of this printing device presupposes the existence (and availability) of paper, a substance we moderns feel buried in.

Today Westerners are fond of putting down the people who live in what we label "developing countries." Ironically, I'd guess that one of the reasons we Westerners sometimes feel superior is because we are a paper-driven society. I say "ironically" for a good reason:

A.D. 105	Paper invented in Lei-yang, China.
A.D. 610	Paper introduced to Japan from Korea.
A.D. 751	Paper made in Samarkand.
A.D. 793	Paper is introduced in Bagdad.
A.D. 900	Paper is made in Egypt.
A.D. 1100	Morocco learns papermaking from Egypt.
A.D. 1151	First paper mill in Xativa, Spain, brought over from North Africa by the Arab Moors.
A.D. 1276	Paper manufacturing begins at Fabriano, Italy.
A.D. 1348	Paper mill in Tropes, France.
A.D. 1390	Paper mill started in Nuremburg, Germany.
A.D. 1494	First paper mill in England (Hertfordshire)
A.D. 1690	First paper mill in America (Germantown, PA)

(Peterdi 52.)

Once you are aware of this sequence it makes it a lot easier to understand why we label a certain period "The Dark Ages." Without paper, how was education to take place? And, most mind-boggling of all, China had paper almost a millennium and a half before England had it! And even Japan had it nine centuries before England.

I was so intrigued by the paper chart that it caused me to rethink history in terms of paper, especially the arts. Which obviously led me to the Renaissance. What effect did paper have on it?

A.D. 1151: Paper Comes to Spain

The Moslem Moors brought the full range of the arts to Spain long before that occurred in the rest of Europe. Their centers of learning were renowned everywhere. The Chinese had a virtual monopoly on paper for 600 years, and then the Moslems controlled it for another 500 years. As a graphic illustration of the radical difference between the Arab civilizations and the Christian counterparts, McMurtrie observed that in the eleventh century the Caliph's library in Cairo alone contained 150,000 books, while in Europe it was a rare monastery library that contained more than 150 (McMurtrie 67)! After Ferdinand and Isabella consolidated their hold on Spain in 1492, the non-Moor Renaissance began. Cervantes (1547-1616) started in with the first novel in literature, *Don Quixote*, and was followed by Lope de Vega (1562-1635), José Ribera (1588-1656), Francisco de Zurbaran (1588-1663?), Diego de Valesquez (1599-1660), and Calderon de la Barca (1600-1681).

Unfortunately, Spain committed intellectual suicide. Not content with expelling the Moors and Jews from the peninsula, the despotic monarchy and the Inquisition joined together to hurl the Spanish Empire backward into a cultural abyss.

A.D. 1276: Paper Comes to Italy

Look what happened! It started the Renaissance! Dante (1265-1321), Petrarch (1304-1374), Boccaccio (1313-1375). And it didn't slow down until after Leonardo da Vinci (1452-1519) and Michelangelo (1474-1564).

A.D. 1348: Paper Comes to France

Much of France's art-related explosion came in architecture. But note also the sequence letter-wise: Villon (1431-?), Rabelais (1494?-1553), Montaigne (1553-1592).

A.D. 1390: Paper Comes to Germany

Seven universities were founded in Germany between 1348 and 1400. And in art, in quick succession, came Schongauer (1430-1491), Dürer (1471-1528), and Holbein (1497-1543).

A.D. 1494: Paper Comes to England

What a literary logjam burst when this occurred! Sir Thomas More (1478-1535), Edmund Spenser (1552-1599), Ben Jonson (1553-1567), Francis Bacon (1561-1626), William Shakespeare (1564-1616), Christopher Marlowe (1564-1593), John Donne (1572-1631), and John Milton (1608-1674).

A.D. 1690: Paper Comes to America

Even here, in America, little of literary significance happened until paper came: Benjamin Franklin (1706-1790), Philip Freneau (1752-1832), William Cullen Bryant (1794-1878). Then in a 16-year-period, between 1803 and 1819, were born Emerson, Hawthorne, Longfellow, Poe, Holmes, Thoreau, Lowell, and Melville. Ah, the power of paper!

With this in mind we can see why Western printmaking did not begin until the fifteenth century. The Chinese had already used one of the first types of Western printing, block book, for centuries. Text was carved into planks, and pages were printed from them (printed in reverse so it could be read!). This method continued to be used even after the invention of movable type, because this way the printer didn't quickly use up all the letters in his type box (Wechsler 13, 14).

Westerners frequently recall with pride Johann Gutenberg's invention of the movable type printing press (c. 1440-1450) and assume that 1440 represented the beginning of printing. "Not so!" says McMurtrie. During its Tang Dynasty, which began in A.D. 618, China entered into one of the most glorious periods of art and literature our world has ever known. During this period untold thousands of printed impressions, made from wooden blocks, were made. The earliest known book is a Chinese version of the Buddhist *Diamond Sutra,* now housed the British Museum. It was printed—with a woodcut frontispiece—in 868 A.D. As for movable type, McMurtrie points out that the Chinese were using it *at least four centuries before Gutenburg* (McMurtrie 85-95).

While almost all early Western printing was religious (much of it done by monks), except for playing cards, the subject matter soon expanded to include decorative, historic, satiric, mythological, metaphysical subjects—and most everything else.

In the Medieval world the individual was de-emphasized; self was swallowed up in the mass. Only God deserved name recognition. Untold thousands devoted their lives to creating art in building cathedrals (most of which took centuries to complete), and almost none of them were ever known by name. The same with printmakers. For example, a number of the greatest fifteenth century printmakers we only know by title: Master E.S. (flourished 1440-1467) created about 217 plates and was the first to use initials as a signature (as a guard against imitators). Master of the Amsterdam Cabinet (Master of Hausbach) flourished between 1467 and 1507. Because his medium was drypoint (press-runs had to be short), few of his fine prints have survived. Master F.V.B. (end of the fifteenth century) left behind 59 outstanding plates. Master I.A.M. (c. 1440-c. 1504) left 26 engravings.

But the Renaissance brought with it the rise of individualism. No longer were artists willing to voluntarily surrender their identity. In Italy, for instance, where the Renaissance began, we know that Antonio Pollaiuolo (1429-1498), Florentine painter, sculptor, engraver, and architect, was one of the greatest engravers of his time. (Today his fame rests on his splendid engraving, "The Battle of the Naked Men.") Pollaiuolo's eminent contemporary, Andre Mantegna 1431-1506), is considered by art scholars to be perhaps the finest printmaker Italy ever produced.

In Germany and the Low Countries, besides the aforementioned unnamed masters, two other pre-Dürer artists deserve mention. Martin Schongauer (c. 1430-1491), engraved 115 plates, mostly religious, and stylistically, his work bridges from the Gothic Period to the Renaissance. Israhel van Meckenem (end of fifteenth century) we remember for good and bad reasons. One of the most prolific engravers of his century, about 570 plates are attributed to him. He was also one of the most unscrupulous engravers. Case in point, he doctored a number of Master E.S.'s plates (in spite of the initials), then hawked them under his own name! But the unnamed masters, Schongauer and Van Meckenem, were but the foundation; all significant printmaking really begins with our next artist.

Albrecht Dürer (1471-1528). All superlatives are exhausted in describing the career of this most famous German (actually, his father was Hungarian) artist of all, the Germanic counterpart to Italy's Leonardo da Vinci. He was interested in philosophy, science, arts, and all knowledge. His key early mentors were Wolgemut, Schongauer, and Master of Hausbach. Art historians agree that even now, five centuries later, the technical perfection of his plates have never been equaled. Literally working himself into an early grave, he left behind more than 100 engravings, 250 superb woodcuts,

Gutenberg and his printing press

and more than a thousand drawings. He drew from such a broad spectrum (portraying current events, nightmarish visions, biblical characters, war and destruction, the devil and early death, mythology and mysticism, etc.) that he is impossible to pigeonhole. Unquestionably, he set the pace, the standard, the ideal (an almost unreachable perfection) for all who followed.

Prior to Breughel, we should also note four other eminent artist printmakers. Albrecht Altdorfer (c. 1480-1528), German painter, engraver, and architectural designer, produced about 100 copper engravings and 50 woodcuts. One of the most original artists of his time, he was known for his innovative landscapes. Heinrich Aldegrover (c. 1502-1558), a student of Dürer's, produced about 300 plates during his career. Thanks to his sensitive and effective use of chiaroscuro, he was able to crowd his plates to their limits yet retain unity. One of the key figures of the German Renaissance, Lucas Cranach the Elder (c. 1472-1545), was one of the most original artists of his time, his Medieval mysticism reminding one of Breughel's and Bosch's surreal depictions.

Pieter Breughel the Elder (c. 1520-1569) was one of the great painters of his time. But Breughel was also one of the greatest craftsmen who ever lived, as well as having an encyclopedic vision of his world. According to Longstreet "his prints show us the inner world of his time—phantoms, spooks, sins—as well as landscapes, pleasures, dances, weddings, feasts, games." His people seem overly energized, most likely a natural outgrowth of the short life expectancy of his time (below 20 years). Because of death by war, disease, Black Plague, child-birth complications, infant mortality, etc., very few survived to adulthood. Breughel portrayed those who did as savoring every moment they might have left (Longstreet 36-37).

Six artists of note prior to the next titan ought to be mentioned here. Peterdi considers Lucas Van Leyden (1494-1533) to be "the Mozart of engraving." His most characteristic qualities are his elegant style and use of light. Hans Holbein the Younger (c. 1497-1543), while a renowned painter, was also a splendid draftsman, producing during his career a vast number of woodcut illustrations. Jean Duvet (1485-1561) was one of the most interesting and enigmatic figures in printmaking history, for appreciation of his work did not come until 400 years later! Hercules Seghers (1589-1638) was also misunderstood and unappreciated during his lifetime. His enigmatic yet brilliant work has baffled critics from his age to ours. He was the first to experiment with Intaglio color printing. A student of Rubens, a great painter, and superb draftsman, Anthony Van Dyck (1599-1641) produced some of the finest portrait prints ever created. Like Hogarth, famed French illustrator Jacques Callot (1592-1635) not only recorded customs, historical events, and contemporary morals, but forcefully commented on them via his many prints.

Rembrandt van Rijn (1606-1669), like Dürer, was a titan, considered to be one of the greatest artists this world has known. Besides his famous paintings, this great Dutch artist is considered to be the greatest etcher of all time. Success came early to him, then it turned away from him. Nevertheless, he steered straight ahead, leaving behind a legacy of art far ahead of his time.

Especially is he known for his interplay of light and shadow. There is a glow that appears to emanate from within his characters. Rembrandt is also appreciated because of his vulnerability. He left behind a long series of self-portraits, movingly depicting each stage of his life, from proud young man to battered old sage. Also, he is considered to be one of the greatest of all landscapists. He created 300 of the world's great etchings.

Antonio (Canaletto) Canal (1697-1768) loved Venice and painted it from every angle, in every season, and in every kind of atmosphere. He did the same in his etchings, flooding his prints with light. Although known for his great paintings and frescoes, Giovanni Battista Tiepolo (1696-1770) was also a splendid draftsman, leaving behind 38 etchings. His ability to create luminous space was later built upon by Goya. Another Italian, Giambattista Piranesi (1720-1778), trained as an architect, and it shows. He had a mania for reproducing on prints the grandest Roman buildings that still survived. He completed more than 3,000 etchings during his career. He is best known, however, for his series of 16 prints depicting imaginary prisons, surrealistic nightmares of hells that go nowhere. Longstreet likens him to a strange combination of Kafka, Frank Lloyd Wright, Poe, and Orwell (Longstreet, 96-103).

William Hogarth (1697-1764), born within view of the infamous Newgate Prison in London, grew up in a world veering out of Puritan repression into a world dedicated to pleasure, love of life, dissipation, and decadence. His father, Richard Hogarth, first published Defoe's *Robinson Crusoe*. After sowing his fair share of wild oats, Hogarth married, settled down, and looked for something that might make his fortune. He found it in copper engravings, more specifically in a biting series of moralizing prints that visually read like novels. His first series, "Harlot's Progress," graphically depicted a young innocent's "progress" into prostitution (which was then epidemic in London), and then her total disintegration as a person. That series made him famous overnight. Next came his equally famous "A Rake's Progress" that targeted British high society. In it a young aristocrat runs through his family fortune, and women, and every kind of dissipation, only to end up insane in the infamous Bedlam prison-hospital. "Marriage a la Mode," another series, tackled the upper classes again, this time their little better than prostitution system of arranged marriages (made for purely financial reasons). The emptiness and immoral nature of such a travesty on marriage is vividly portrayed. Another series, "A Consultation of Physicians," dealt with medical quackery. Taken in its entirety, his remarkable social satire portrays a frivolous society dancing on the edge of a precipice (some fascinating similarities to our own age).

Francisco Jose de Goya y Lucientes (1746-1828) was another titan, one of the towering figures in European art. He grew up in a Spain that had lost its greatness, its vitality, its soul. In this society, decadent and dissolute almost beyond belief, the Inquisition still sought out heretics to torture or burn. The royal family had intermarried to the point of incestuousness, and family insanity was wreaking havoc throughout the empire. Goya, as dissolute as any of them, nevertheless managed to hold on to his conscience. Over time, he used his paintings, and especially his prints, to preach judgment to the Spanish people. No one was immune to his scathing indictments. Anticipating the amoral world of Freudian thought, the world his prints depicted was one governed by social expediency and helplessness in an inexorable system where the spirit of God has seemingly departed. His great series of "Disaster of War" prints is unmatched, even by Picasso's "Guernica." Longstreet notes of it, "No artist before or since has pictured so perfectly the madness and futility of human warfare" (Longstreet 104-127).

William Blake (1757-1827) lived in an entirely different world from that of Goya. Poet, engraver, philosopher, inventor, mystic, printer, publisher, symbolist, visionary, and semi mad at times, Blake defies description. No one was like him before his time, and no one after. The Old Testament world was to him far more vivid than anything in the external British world. From Scripture and from Michelangelo, Raphael, and Gothic art, he created a cosmography uniquely his own. Inspiration, he felt, was the only true revelation. He spent all he had on his incredible prints, and lived and died virtually unknown. In fact, tragically, so misunderstood was he that over 100 volumes of his texts and drawings were burned after his death as "inventions of the devil!" (Longstreet 154-164).

On a separate track completely from the western counterpart, in far away, virtually unknown Japan, things were happening that would have a seismic impact on the rest of the world's perception of art. Hanabusa Itcho (1652-1724) is considered to be one of Japan's greatest satirical artists. So biting was his print-carried satire that he was banished for 12 years. Okumura Masanobu (1689-1756), one of the most important Japanese innovators, invented the two-color print and standardized color printing. Toshusai Sharaku (flourished in 1793) is one of the art world's great enigmas. Though unknown as a person, even today his magnificent portrayals of Japan's 300 greatest actors—bold, psychological, rich in color—were so far ahead of time that when Impressionist painters later discovered them, the art world rocked. Kitagawa Utamaro (c. 1754-1806) is considered to be the great poet of Japanese art. No more tenderhearted Japanese artist ever lived. During his aborted career he searched for beauty in all things and produced more than 600 series of print books and albums. He was jailed at age 50 for one print that offended someone, and died with a broken heart shortly after his release. Katsushika Hokusai (1760-1849) is considered to be perhaps the greatest woodcut artist who ever lived, producing more than 35,000 drawings and prints during his long career—*besides* writing books and poetry. Few masters in art history can compare in variety and depth; his interests were broad and encyclopedic. Like Goya, he started out a classicist and ended up an innovator. Longstreet noted that he was so restless that he lived in about 100 different houses and changed his name more than 30 times! He it was who created the Japanese landscape school around 1795 after falling in love with the European copper etching. He it was who also immortalized the average Japanese citizen, creating, in effect, an Oriental Everyman. Utagawa Ando Hiroshige (1797-1858) is considered to be the last great landscape painter-printmaker Japan has produced. The first great Japanese artist to be appreciated in Europe, and America, he is known for his spontaneity and unique ability to capture fleeting moments in life. During his lifetime, he created more than 5,000 remarkable prints, "The 53 Stages of Tokaido Road" being his most famous series. Longstreet observes that in his work you can actually feel "the fury of the wind, the slanting beat of rain, the feather softness of snow" (Longstreet 193).

Back in the West, Jean Baptiste Camille Corot (1796-1875), although known as one of France's greatest landscape painters, also produced some of the nineteenth century's finest landscape prints. Mystic, symbolist, and surrealist Odilon Redon (1840-1916) produced 206 superb graphic works, mostly etchings, with some lithographs. Edouard Manet (1832-1883) produced 75 etchings and 20 some lithographs. Next to Degas, he was the finest draftsman in the Impressionist School. Hilaire Germain Edgar Degas (1834-1917), while his knowledge of etching was shaky, nevertheless produced a number of magnificent prints.

One of the greatest political satirists in the history of graphic art, Honore Daumier (1808-1879), was the first major artist to work almost exclusively in lithography. He explored and exploited that medium to its fullest in more than 4,000 lithograph prints. Daumier, Longstreet maintains, is the art counterpart to Balzac in literature, the champion of the average man or woman, and the critic of "the flabby world of material success and ladder-climbing." Under the comic masks of his multitudinous characters, Daumier pointed out and ridiculed all the wrongs of his time, managing to somehow incorporate sympathy and understanding (Longstreet 200-204).

Only two Americans make it into the rarified atmosphere of the world's great print creators. James McNeil Whistler (1834-1903), transplanted to London, never became all he could have been, choosing rather to become a celebrity by what he did and what he said. Nevertheless, along the way he became captivated by the Japanese woodcuts and etched some magnificent prints of his own, especially his "Dock and Riverside" series and his "Nocturne" series. He freely admitted that he owed his knowledge of composition and color to Japanese prints. He had one art-related objective: to somehow reconcile reality and imagination (Longstreet 216-226). Winslow Homer (1836-1910), on the other hand, stayed home. Today he is considered by many to be America's most original native artist. Growing up in the waning days of America's Romantic Period, he was in for a rude awakening during America's Civil War. A war correspondent for *Harper's Weekly*, he created woodcut illustrations wherever he went. These, often appearing as one- or two-page spreads in *Harpers*, along with Matthew Brady's photographs, constituted most of the visual perceptions Americans had of that war. Unlike other woodcut artists, Homer concentrated (as Ernie Pyle and Bill Mauldin would do in later wars) on the average American soldier, not on officers or heroics. Homer too was deeply impressed by Japanese woodcuts. After the war he went to New York and recorded street life there. A rugged Thoreau, he soon tired of urban life and spent the rest of his life on his beloved New England coast, and the seacoast was virtually his only subject the rest of his life, both in his paintings and in his prints.

Paul Gaughin (1848-1903) believed the artist must be true to himself, impose order on disorder, set up rational boundaries beyond which not to go, and to free himself to achieve the impossible. Disliking Europe, he sought out a Shangri-la in the South Pacific. But Longstreet maintains that his private universe was closer to William Blake than to Tahiti. Few artists of our age have had a more powerful impact on the world's perception of art than Gaughin exerted through his simplistic paintings and hand-made woodcuts. Using color sparingly, his prints were really monoprints. His two-dimensional art represented a return to the simplicity of the Middle Ages. *Everything is cyclical* (Longstreet 238-248)!

Obviously, this may be considered an odd place to stop, for after Gaughin came many other famous artists who achieved greatness in their prints, artists such as Toulouse-Lautrec, Edvard Munch, James Ensor, Edward Hopper, Howard Pyle, Georges Rouault, Henri Matisse, Joan Miró, Marc Chagall, and (most influential of all, painting and print wise) Pablo Picasso. Nevertheless, with Gaughin representing the full circle closing of a half-millennium-long cycle, I chose to conclude this modest study with Gaughin.

Now you can see what I meant earlier. In truth, the woodcuts and kindred forms of illustration that grace the *Christmas in My Heart* anthologies represent not the fringe of great world art, as I had always assumed, but are as central a form of expression as painting itself!

The Illustrations We Use

I can almost hear you pose the question: "True enough, the woodcut has an illustrious past, but what about the ones *you* use? Do *they?*" I'd have to temporize, "I really don't know."

Actually, what we use most is akin to the fifteenth century Old Masters: just as was true then, rarely do I know who the woodcut illustrator was that I use. I wish I did! Woodcuts were kind of a commodity during the nineteenth century. I am likely to find a given woodcut illustration showing up in a dozen different children's books, as well as in a number of different magazines. In other words, authors and editors bought the rights to use certain very special illustrations. Some were printed on what was then state-of-the-art printing presses. Others were not (and the differences are obvious!). Certainly the relative quality of the paper used made a real difference (an even greater difference as time passed by).

Nevertheless, even though I don't currently know who the artists were, I am going to keep searching, for some of the artists who made them did such wonderful work, covering the full range of emotions—laughter to tears; slapstick to pathos; joy to tragedy—that their names *ought* to be remembered.

The Seventh Collection

Well, here we are, six years later, and *Christmas in My Heart* is chugging along with a greater head of steam than it has ever had in the past. So, clearly, thousands of families have gathered its stories to their hearts and interwoven them in their family Christmas traditions and daily story hour during the Advent and the Twelve Days of Christmas. For all this, we humbly thank you.

For this seventh collection we have brought back Arthur Gordon (you will remember his "Miraculous Staircase" story last year); Carolyn Rathbun-Sutton ("Under the Banana Leaf Christmas Tree," in *Christmas in My Heart*, 5); Eric Philbrook Kelly ("The Christmas Nightingale," in *Christmas in My Heart*, 3); and Grace Richmond ("On Christmas Day in the Morning," in *Christmas in My Heart*, 4). "New" authors we are introducing this year include turn-of-the-century writers Minnie Leona Upton, A. May Holaday, and Frederick Hall. And we are also introducing five contemporary writers: Elizabeth Orton Jones, Anita L. Fordyce, Virginia Everett Davidson, Lissa Halls Johnson, and Nancy N. Rue. A stellar mix, if we've ever had one!

The write-in story of the year? Without question, "When Tad Remembered"! *And* I prophesy that some of the stories written by living authors that we are featuring will go on to achieve classic status in the Christmas genre. Which those will be, I leave up to you.

Coda

I look forward to hearing from you! Please do keep the stories, responses, and suggestions coming. And not just for Christmas stories. I'm putting together collections centered around other genres as well. You may reach me by writing to:

Joe L. Wheeler, Ph.D.
c/o Review and Herald® Publishing Association
55 West Oak Ridge Drive
Hagerstown, MD 21740

Red Shoes

Anita L. Fordyce

In almost every day's mail we get stories: stories that are merely stories, stories that are a cut above average, stories that are memorable enough to include in one of our collections, and stories that put us out of commission—as is the case with this story. After picking up our mail on our way out of town on a trip, Connie opened the packet, pulled out this true story, was intrigued by the title, and began reading it out loud.

We almost had to stop the car!

Christmas Eve day dawned, a Currier and Ives sort of day, with a wet, soft snow. Normally, snow, especially for Christmas, lightened my spirits; but not today. All night long I had continually rehearsed my 5-year-old daughter, Jeney's, questions.

"Why did God give me crippled feet? Special shoes don't make them any better. Why can't I wear shoes like other girls wear?"

I had no answers, only the belief that God doesn't make mistakes. But she couldn't understand. Jeney had a condition called hypermobile feet, aggravated by poorly developed leg muscles and rheumatoid arthritis. More than flat, they turned over at the ankles. Her doctor said there was a possible corrective surgery, but for now orthopedic shoes would be best. The surgery, he cautioned, would permanently fuse her feet and give her stiff ankles for the rest of her life.

"I hate the shoes!" she cried. "They are ugly and always brown—brown, like boys wear."

They were always bulky, too, in order to accommodate an orthotic—a special ankle brace. In early December her doctor had given her a new shoe prescription. We usually ordered them from a shoe store, but this time we had been recommended to a semiretired shoemaker in our little New England village. He hand stitched specialty shoes for only a select few customers, so getting him to consider us hadn't been easy.

At a prearranged time we entered his dusty workshop that doubled as an antique shop. The only thing to remind us of the coming holiday was a large sleigh bell that jingled when the door shut behind us. The shoemaker, a large man with silver hair, was sitting at an oversized sewing machine in the back of a cluttered shop. He acknowledged our entrance with a cursory look over the top of half glasses that looked like the spectacles one pictured Santa Claus wearing. It was obvious we were to wait.

Finally, he laid down his work and slowly rose, steadying his balance upon the arm of the sewing machine. We were shocked to see him hobble toward us. Our eyes automatically dropped to his large, obviously deformed feet shrouded in odd-shaped black shoes. He stood in front of us only a few seconds. Out of breath, he sat down on the edge of a large flat table and looked down at my high heeled shoes.

"You'll ruin your feet," he said in a raspy voice.

"We're here to talk about new shoes for Jeney," I said, gathering my courage. Intimidated, Jeney had ducked around my back. I took her hand and drew her out to face the tired man. "Her doctor has given us a new shoe prescription, and we're told you make the best."

"It's the holidays, you know." He ignored my compliment and waved away my hand as I attempted to hand him the prescription. "I couldn't possibly make anything until January."

"I don't want new shoes anyway," Jeney spoke up in an insolent tone that betrayed her distaste for shoes, *any* shoes.

"Take your shoes off," he barked and gestured for me to put her on the table where he was sitting. "Let me see your feet." Lifting her up to sit beside him, I began to undo her laces. She brushed my hands away and pulled the tied shoes off. They dropped to the floor with a thud, and her orthotics fell out.

The shoemaker moved a crumpled piece of brown wrapping paper toward her and smoothed it out. "Here, stand on this," he said gruffly.

Obediently, she stood up and placed her white-socked feet on the paper. Deftly, he ran his fingers around the edge of each foot and with a pencil drew their outline. Wordlessly, he sucked in his breath, looked up at the ceiling, and then at the outline on the paper that remained after Jeney stepped aside. Tears brimmed on his eyelids.

"She's got a serious problem, doesn't she?" he said to me in a much softer voice. Still sitting, he reached up and put his hands around her waist to place her back on

the table's edge. With no further comment, he then took each foot in his hands and examined their shape, appearing to memorize them.

"Jeney," he said directly to her, "you and I have something in common."

"What?"

"We have painful feet."

"How did you know that?" she asked with wide blue eyes.

He ignored her question. "You hate shoes too."

"How did you know that?" she repeated.

"Do you see my shoes?" he pointed to the floor. "My feet were like yours when I was a little boy. But they became crippled because there were no helpful shoes or surgery for me. That is why I now make special shoes for special people."

I hoped that the man's personal, rather than clinical, interest in her would be helpful, but Jeney wasn't impressed. She looked away from his feet to her own.

"Let me see her prescription." He reached out his hand toward the paper I was still holding. "This is correct," he said, and tilted Jeney's face to look into his own. She continued to look down with her eyes and swung her feet in a circular motion. Dangling above the floor, they showed no hint of impediment.

"Let's go pick out some leather for your shoes," he said. Without allowing her to refuse, he slowly stood and lifted her off the table, set her on the floor, took her by the hand, and walked toward a darkened, closet-like room. "What color would you like your shoes to be?" I heard him ask her as they both hobbled away, she still in her sock feet. It was obvious I wasn't to go with them, but I was able to see her almost eagerly choose a piece of red leather.

Still hand-in-hand, they came back to the front of the store while he explained that the shoes would have to be the usual oxford style with laces. It would be six to eight weeks before they could be ready. Even though less defiant, Jeney still didn't say much, but she reached up, took the leather from him, and deliberately put it beside the brown paper with the outline of her feet traced on it.

Red or not, breaking in new orthopedic shoes would be difficult. I was grateful that we would not get them until after the holidays. So when the shoemaker called on December 23 to say he had gotten her shoes done, I was sick, especially when he insisted on seeing her at noon on Christmas Eve day. However, because there was an excited tone in his voice—so different from our first meeting—I couldn't tell him that the shoes would ruin Christmas.

When we told Jeney the shoes were ready, her spirits dropped. Red or not, nothing we said removed the agony of facing another pair of orthopedic shoes, even a promise that she didn't have to begin wearing them until after Christmas Day.

When the day of the appointment arrived, I made excuses not to go. It was difficult to mask my emotion as I watched her daddy help her into her red snowsuit and stocking cap. *If only she could be as bright as the Christmas color she is wearing,* I thought as she trudged out the door.

More than an hour passed. The shop was only a mile from our house. It should have been a 15-minute trip. The snow continued to fall, and while I tried to keep busy, I could only sit numbly by a window and watch the mounting whiteness.

"God," I finally begged, "somehow give her a blessing for Christmas. Let her know You care. We try to believe that it was not a mistake when You gave her special feet. But she has such a hard time with the shoes . . ."

Thumping footsteps on the porch interrupted my prayer. I braced myself with a big smile and started for the door. But before I could get there, Jeney shoved the door open wide, whirling snow to her back. She had a smile that was brighter than her red snowsuit, and she was skipping—almost dancing.

"Mommy! Look! Look!" she squealed.

I couldn't believe my eyes. Shining out from the cuffs of her snowsuit pants were shiny red shoes, designed in a princess style, with a strap and a brass buckle! She danced around the room like a ballerina. Her feet didn't turn over the sides of the shoes. It was easy to see that the shoes were as functional as the usual oxford style, but very comfortable. She had never been able to wear anything like them. It was a miracle! *How had it happened?*

"It was the shoemaker, Mommy," she said simply, reading my thought. "He said God told him how to make them just for me. He made them for me, for church tonight. Look! They're just like other girls wear!"

My husband explained that after the shoemaker had taken impressions of her feet, he had ingeniously fashioned a functional orthopedic shoe with the proper heel and instep and, amazingly, with room for her or-thotic insert. This prevented her feet from turning over. Then, with an understanding heart, the shoemaker had designed a princess style.

For Jeney the shoes were the greatest gift she had ever received. She learned through the shoemaker that God cared about her heartache and wanted to ease her suffering. My faith too was strengthened as I agreed that truly God had put it upon the shoemaker's heart to understand her needs.

We remember the red shoes every Christmas, and we've kept them in a box of family treasures. However, with the years came the realization that shoes were not going to correct the problem; surgery ultimately was unavoidable. As she grew older, walking became exhausting and more painful. Running and physical activity were almost an impossibility. We found, too, that surgical methods had changed, and her feet would not be permanently fused. After many years and dozens of pairs of shoes and orthotics, Jeney had two corrective surgeries. Today, she not only wears shoes "like other girls wear," but also has feet "like other girls have."

According to freelance writer, editor, and teacher, Anita Fordyce, "Jeney Ann is today the mother of two sons and walks with straight legs on the path she believes the Lord is showing her. To our knowledge, the shoemaker is now dead; however, his heartfelt concern and love taught Jeney a valuable lesson and gave her a reason to keep trying. Eventually, a Christian doctor at Temple Sports Medicine in Philadelphia surgically gave her 'new' feet. When he saw her for the first time he said, 'You've done everything there is to do.'"

Feliz Navidad!

Carolyn Rathbun-Sutton

Nothing was going right, nothing had gone right, and it seemed probable that nothing ever would go right that "bad-hair-day" Christmas Eve.

Since Carolyn Rathbun's memorable story,"Under the Banana Leaf Christmas Tree," was published in Christmas in My Heart, *book 5, she married a rancher and moved to Oregon, where she now lives and writes in a mountainous area not far from Grants Pass.*

It was the afternoon of Christmas Eve, and I was having a "bad hair day"! I pushed open the door to Connie and Friends hair salon. Actually, to put it bluntly, I'd been having a bad hair year. The divorce I thought would never happen to me was almost final. I was feeling worthless, depleted on every level, and—most of all—ugly. *Really* ugly.

Oh, sure, I'd still be "celebrating" Christmas with my family: that's Mom *with* Dad; brother *with* wife; aunt *with* uncle; and son *with* girlfriend. I, on the other hand, would *not* be part of a couple—for the first time in 23 years.

And as if that weren't painful enough, probation had just run out for my last permanent wave. In the late December fog my hair looked like a stringy mop. Ugly! All the beauty shops I'd called in the southern California town where my parents lived were fully booked. Only Connie and Friends, 'way down the street, could take me.

Warm air, rancid with the odor of a dozen strong hair chemicals, struck my face as the door swung closed behind me. Static-punctuated mariachi music blared through scratched wooden speakers hanging precariously on the wall next to an inexpensive foil banner reading "Feliz Navidad!"

This is just great! I thought sarcastically. *The one year I really need a little holiday cheer I end up in "Little Mexico"!*

A short, middle-aged Hispanic woman approached me, Christmas-ornament earrings peeking out from under her short-cropped, peroxide-blond hair.

Don't tell me I'm gonna leave here looking like that! I thought.

"I'm Connie," said the woman with a thick accent and warm smile. She extended her hand. I shook it. "How can I help you?" she asked, as if she really meant it.

Well, for starters, I wanted to say, *you can put my marriage back together for me.* But instead I answered, "I have an appointment for a permanent at 4:00."

A quick glance told me I was the only non-Hispanic in the shop. I followed Connie toward the shampoo bowls. On the way, we passed low tables strewn with back issues of *The National Enquirer,* three customers lost in magazine reading under hair dryers, and two other beauticians hard at work on clients' holiday hair-do's.

But it was the big, wavy-haired man with five-o'clock shadow seated on a stool in the corner that I wasn't expecting to see. Totally out of context in a beauty salon—and totally oblivious to what was going on around him—he plucked away at an old guitar.

When I did a double take, Connie explained, "That's Pico, Maria's husband. They only have one car, and he works an early shift on Thursdays. So he comes here and waits for her until she's finished with her customers."

Except for Connie's pleasant patter in two languages (which gave me tacit permission to check out, mentally), the next hour was sheer misery. Dozens of sticky green curlers pulled tightly at my head. Cold, smelly solution ran down my scalp. And I kept getting hopelessly lost in a bank of dark mental clouds with no silver lining.

At one unidentifiable point during this hour someone shut off the mariachi music, and I began hearing strains of Pico's guitar. I had to admit he had a rather nice voice—and an amazing repertoire. For someone playing in a beauty shop, anyway. I had to give him credit for being so sweet and patient about waiting for Maria. She looked tired, if not a bit haggard, for her obviously young years. Things must be tough for them. But hey! Times were tough for all of us—especially for *me* right now!

Connie's cheerful voice roused me from my heavy thoughts. "Time to come to the shampoo bowl. It won't be long now."

I glanced outside. It was dark already. Getting out of my chair, I noticed that all but one other client had gone. Maria was sweeping the floor by her work station. In a half-hearted effort to manifest the Christmas spirit, despite my *bah-humbug!* state of mind, I mumbled to Pico as I passed, "Your music sounds good."

Almost as soon as Connie started rinsing the solution out of my hair, Pico rolled his stool to the other side of the shampoo bowl, guitar in hand. "What kind of music do you like, uh, —"

"My name's Carolyn," I said, suddenly wishing I hadn't complimented him.

"Pico," he introduced himself, pushing his hand

into one of mine. "I'm Maria's husband. What kind of music do you like?"

"It really doesn't matter," I answered. I spoke truthfully, for *nothing* mattered much anymore.

"Well, then, here's a little ballad Elvis Presley came out with in the late 50s—Or was it the early 60s?" Pico strummed once to get the key and started tapping his foot before beginning with a characteristic Presley growl. "'It'll be a [pause] bu-*lue* [tap, tap, tap] Cuh-*ris*-mas [tap] without you.'"

The lyrics should have depressed me, but the thought of personalized live entertainment at the shampoo bowl on Christmas Eve somehow got in the way. The weirdness of the whole thing sort of buoyed me up.

"Country!" Pico guessed excitedly, when he'd finished the Elvis song. "I'll bet you like country." Before I could respond, Pico cleared his throat. "This one was recorded smack in the folksong era. It's called 'Cottonfields,' and it climbed right to the top of the charts."

"Yeah, I know that one," I answered, in spite of myself. Then I volunteered, "I sang harmony on it years ago with a folk group at a youth camp one summer."

"Great!" he said. "I hope you'll still enjoy it!"

He tapped his foot and enthusiastically exploded, "Two . . . three . . . four . . . 'When I was a little, bitty baby, my mama would rock me in the cradle. . . .'"

Maria, finished now with her cleanup, had pulled on her coat and was standing behind Pico, ready to go. The third beautician brought the other customer to the bowl beside mine. I couldn't get over the fact that everyone in here acted as if this scenario were a *normal,* everyday occurrence! The whole thing was so ludicrous

that for a minute I honestly didn't care how ugly I looked or how bad I hurt.

Maybe that's why I did one of the most uncharacteristic things I've ever done. With those green rollers pushing into my neck from the pressure of the shampoo bowl, and with neutralizer dripping from my soggy hair, I simply relaxed, took a deep breath, and belted out in a loud alto, "'But when those cottonballs get rotten, you can't pick very much cotton. . . .'"

"Oooh!" cooed the other customer, beginning to snap her fingers. Connie put down the rinsing hose and clapped in time to the guitar's rhythm. When we finished, everyone cheered and applauded.

When Connie led me back to her work station, Pico and Maria followed, situating themselves to our right. Soon the other customer was seated in the adjacent chair to our left. In the mirror I watched as Connie blew a new style into my hair—and maybe a dark thought or two out of my head.

"Feliz Navidad," Pico suggested, and burst into song once again. This preceded "O Little Town of Bethlehem" and "God Rest Ye Merry Gentlemen" in Spanish. The others now openly hummed along or harmonized.

Then the shop fell silent except for the heater snapping the little foil "Feliz Navidad" banner against the wall. As Connie gave final spurts of spray to my bangs, Pico said, "Before she goes, let's all sing a song that Carolyn can sing with us. We've got her trapped right in the middle of us anyway."

With that, he strummed once and took a deep breath. "'Silent Night . . .'" His rich baritone voice filled and sweetened the very air. Standing behind him, Maria put her arms lightly about his neck. Then she gave me a weary smile and added her soft harmony. "'Holy Night . . .'" I was about to join in when Connie leaned over, gave one final flick to the back of my newly-permed hair, and whispered, "You look beautiful!"

"'All is calm,'" the others sang.

Then I heard my own wavery voice join in with "'All is bright.'"

Connie slipped an arm around my shoulder and, at that very instant, so did Someone else. Someone else Who told me I was beautiful. Someone else Who would be my partner—not only on that Christmas Eve, but on every Christmas Eve until He comes back to take me home for the really big Celebration.

They all shook my hand when I got up to leave.

"Can you come back again next Thursday?" asked Maria.

"No," I answered, "I'll be home by then."

"Too bad!" said Pico, playfully accenting his broad smile with a quick guitar strum.

The last thing I called out over my shoulder to Connie and friends was, "Merry Christmas!"

In chorus, they answered, "Feliz Navidad!"

I walked through the door, out into the gray Christmas Eve fog, but my heart was singing, "'All is bright!'"

Who knows? I thought. *Maybe I am in for a "good hair year" after all.*

How Far Is It to Bethlehem?

Elizabeth Orton Jones

Reenactments of the Nativity have taken place for centuries—who knows how many thousands of times? Chances are, however, that none have been more unique or moving than that put on by the children of the Crotched Mountain Rehabilitation Center in Greenfield, New Hampshire, many years ago.

After considerable sleuthing, I tracked down not just the rehabilitation center itself (it is still there), but the writer/artist, winner of the prestigious Caldecott Award for her artwork in Rachel Field's childhood classic, Prayer for a Child, *and author/artist of other childhood classics, such as* Maminka's Children, Twig, David, *and* Ragman of Paris.

She told me how, while painting murals on the walls of this wonderful center (supported by New Hampshire's Society for Crippled Children and Handicapped Persons), some of the children came up to her late one fall and asked whether it was possible for them to be in a nativity play. Because of their serious physical disabilities, they had all been excluded from such a Christmas event. This true story tells what followed. So indelibly did that nativity enactment impress her that she wrote it down for Boston's Horn Book Magazine, *and later published it as a Christmas book, complete with her own silhouette illustrations.*

Although nearly half a century has passed since that first nativity play in 1953, it continues to be a yearly tradition to reenact it each Christmas, there in the snow-capped mountains of New Hampshire.

Once each year the whole world of us becomes a child begging for his favorite story, longing, through the telling, to go again to his favorite place—a quiet, humble, hay-filled place where gentle creatures are—ox, ass, and sheep, shepherds and kneeling kings, a Mother and a newborn Babe. It is the stable at Bethlehem, under the Star. At the time of the gathering of seasonal shadows, at the dusk of the year, when the darkest days are upon us and the winter's chill, we seek inner light from this Star, spiritual warmth and strength within this place. "Tell me the Christmas Story," begs the child.

Here, there, and everywhere it is told, in many ways, with many interpretations. Sometimes the telling is of straw, sometimes of gold. Sometimes it is covered with so thick an overlay of festivity and accompanied by such a cacophony of commercialistic sound that the child feels weary and lost, unable to find what he is seeking. "How far is it to Bethlehem?" he asks. The tellings he treasures are those that contain the answer: "Not very far."

* * *

Such a telling took place one Sunday before Christmas in a rehabilitation center for crippled children high on a New Hampshire mountainside. People came from far and wide to see the children give a Christmas play. An audience of about 200 crowded into the library there, stood along the corridor, and even outdoors in the snow where they could look through a large window at the scene within. A roughly-painted backdrop of the night sky over Bethlehem hung at one end of the room, surrounded with branches of pine and hemlock from the woods. A big, slightly unsymmetrical gold-foil star, sprinkled generously with bottled glitter, was suspended from the ceiling by a wire. A rather crooked dove of peace cut from white paper swayed ever so slightly in the air above a baby's battered playpen piled high with hay from a kind farmer's barn. A corrugated-cardboard ox and ass, with tails of raveled rope, were propped up, one at the right, the other at the left. Two boys from a neighboring town, proud to have been appointed "stage hands" by the crippled children, stood at attention behind the curtains at each side. Only their legs and feet could be seen.

The audience sat, or stood, in a respectful sort of silence, waiting to see and hear the Story told by children who were unable to walk, many of whom were unable to talk, all of them deprived, in large measure, of what is usually taken for granted as the rightful heritage of every child born on earth.

At a sign, the two stage hands behind the curtains walked on tiptoe toward each other, pulling the curtains together. A sound of singing was heard from far down the corridor behind the closed door to the wards. The door opened. The singing grew louder, came nearer, as, slowly—in wheelchairs, on crutches, and in the arms of nurses—the procession of crippled children approached. It mattered not whether they could carry a tune or re-

spond to a definite rhythm; it mattered not whether they could pronounce words. They *sang*, "O Come, All Ye Faithful, Joyful and Triumphant!" Triumphant indeed, they came. The manner of locomotion mattered not a bit. In truth, they all came on wings to their giving, the first experience of its sort any of them had ever known. Joyful indeed was this occasion, principally because it was their own idea—their very own. It had arisen out of heartfelt gratitude. No one had suggested to them that a Christmas play might be an interesting and an appropriate thing for them to do.

"We want to give a Christmas play!" they had said, speaking slowly, first one and then another, one evening after supper when they were all in the library, several months before. "With Mary, and Joseph, and the Christ Child, and the animals, and the kings, and the Star—everything, just like in the Bible. We want to do it *all ourselves*. So much has been done for us."

At the head of the procession, wrapped in a clean crib sheet wound with a blue ribbon, a little boy was carried—a 3-year-old, but still a baby. Stiff in his locked braces, he looked very like the Bambino in an old medieval Italian nativity. The expression of calm delight on his small, pale face, as he turned his head to smile at all the people, told that he knew Who he was. For more than a week he had been laid in the manger, a little while each day, so that he would not be frightened when the real occasion came. Gradually, he had learned to feel as much at home in the manger, between the ox and the ass, as in his own crib. "You are our Christ Child!" the others had told him, gently, over and over and over.

Following him came a girl of 14 in her wheelchair,

wearing a dress of blue, trimmed at the front with two stars and a large M shaped from shiny silver ribbon and stitched painstakingly by many small, halting hands. "This must be *especially* pretty, because this is for our Mary!" the children had said. A large lace-paper doily painted gold was fastened to the white shawl she wore on her head. So misshapen in body was she that her family had never taken her anywhere, for fear of her being seen. Now there was beauty of a breathtaking quality about her as, eyes uplifted, noticing the people not at all, she kept repeating to herself in a soft, awed whisper, *"I—am—Mary!"*

A boy wearing a brown robe and a brown skullcap, to which had been attached a brown yarn beard and a large gold halo just like Mary's, was Joseph, calm and dignified, though there had been moments of complete revolt, tears, and endless repetitions of "I can't! I just can't!" followed later by fits of uncontrollable giggles every time the beard was tried on.

Half a dozen little boys followed, all wearing headpieces encircled with braided black yarn. These were the shepherds. Two of them were in wheelchairs, one on crutches, the others in the arms of nurses. The two in the wheelchairs carried canes for crooks.

The heavenly host, in long cheesecloth dresses with sashes of shiny ribbon, necklaces of twinkling tinsel, and silvered doily halos, came next in wheelchairs to which had been tied huge, translucent plastic wings, sprayed with artificial snow to make them look "all feathery."

"Sing, choirs of angels . . ."

Singing, they passed behind the closed curtains, one by one. All but the Prophet, who came last, pushed slowly and carefully by two quite small "helping" angels in braces, because he was unable to maneuver his chair himself. He was dressed all in white with a long white yarn beard and an expression that might have been painted by Michelangelo. He was the oldest boy and the only one who could read. He had a deep rich voice, though fatigue and loss of control of his breath often troubled him. "I will speak so that the farthest mountain will hear me," he had declared. "I am the Prophet, telling of the coming of a whole new world. With such beautiful words to say, how could I grow tired or lose my breath?" His "helping" angels pushed him to the center of the closed curtains, turned his chair, opened his scroll and held it for him, looking over his shoulders with admiration as he, in his loudest, deepest voice, read:

"Behold, upon the mountains, the feet of him that bringeth good tidings, that publisheth peace. The Lord God will come with strong hand: he shall gather the lambs . . . and carry them in his bosom. . . . Then shall the eyes of the blind be opened, and the ears of the deaf shall be unstopped. Then shall the lame man leap as an hart and the tongue of the dumb sing. . . . And the crooked shall be made straight and the rough places plain, and all flesh shall see it together."

The curtains parted. A large screen had been placed in front of the manger scene, to represent Mary's house. Mary, in her wheelchair, sat reading her Bible beside a little table. A potted geranium was on the table, and the children's pet parakeet, in his cage, talking sweetly to Mary, tipping and cocking his head, while she reverently read.

Suddenly, given a push by a nurse behind the curtain, the angel Gabriel coasted in unto Mary in such a way as would cause anyone to wonder "what manner of salutation this should be," holding a lily with long gold stamens, fashioned from a paper drinking cup, and saying: "Fear not, Mary: for thou hast found favour with God."

Mary, crossing her hands upon her breast, said, with more meaning than is usually felt by the actress so honored as to have been given the Virgin's part: "Be it unto me according to thy word."

And as the angel departed from her, the heavenly host behind the curtains sang softly, as if Mary were dreaming:

"Shall I tell you who will come to Bethlehem on Christmas Morn, who will kneel them gently down before the Lord, newborn?"* while Mary glorified God and wondered how it would be to bring forth a son who would be called "the Son of the Highest."

The curtains slowly closed. Presently, they parted to show the shepherds abiding in the field before the same large screen, the table now having been removed. The two who were able to sit up kept watch over the flock: three toy lambs and a cardboard sheep. The other shepherds lay as if they were asleep. The angel Gabriel appeared as before, and the shepherds were truly startled, as this appearance had been kept, purposely, a secret from them. And when the whole heavenly host was suddenly with the angel in the same miraculous manner, the amazed shepherds stared wide-eyed and open-mouthed, and kept staring as the "multitude" praised God in proudly learned unison, saying: "Glory to God in the highest, and on earth peace, good will to men!"

Once more the curtains slowly closed, then parted. The screen had been removed and the shepherds, now on their stomachs, truly prostrate before the manger, lifted their heads to see the Child within. Mary, in her wheelchair, sat beside the ox; Joseph, in his, beside the ass. The two "helping" angels stood behind the manger, while the heavenly host watched from all around.

"Where am I now?" asked a little shepherd who was blind.

"Shh!" whispered Mary, leaning down to quiet him by touching his shoulder.

"You're at Bethlehem now."

He smiled, feeling for the hay beside him. Then, reaching into the manger, he found the Christ Child's tiny hand and held it tight.

The Child, making sounds of pure delight, looked up at the ox and the ass, at the "helping" angels smiling down at him, at Joseph, at Mary, who reached over and lovingly caressed his face. One of the shepherds pushed a black lamb over the hay, as if it were walking, until it was close to him. Holding the lamb with one tiny hand and, with the other, the hand of the shepherd who was blind, the Child, giving a sigh of deep satisfaction, looked up at the dove swaying ever so slightly, as if it were truly hovering. He liked to watch it. He did not move. Comfort and joy, peace and sweetness filled a few minutes with a feeling of infinity. One of the heavenly host, a girl who could not speak, gently waved a small braced hand and began humming "Silent Night." As the others joined in the humming, then softly sang the words, many who sat in the audience felt closer to Bethlehem than they had ever felt before.

The coming of the first king was rather astonishing. Wearing his huge crown, resplendent with Christmas tree "jewels," his cotton flannel ermine, and his royal red robe, maneuvering his chair so slowly and quietly through the audience that no one noticed him until he was almost there, he seemed to have come too soon. As a matter of fact, he had come a long, weary way—all the way from the wards, turning the wheel of his chair with one hand while, with the other, he pointed to the Star. Now began the music: "We Three Kings of Orient Are." He approached the manger to present his gift: gold, symbol of the material world. In his green velvet bag was a surprise; he was the only one who knew. Instead of a few little round pieces of cardboard, there was chocolate gold, the kind that is wrapped in foil and stamped, that looks *very* real. So eager was he to have Mary see, that he upturned the bag, filling her lap with the pieces of gold.

"Frankincense to offer have I . . ." Very serious, very erect because of his braced back, the second king came, wheeled by a nurse. His gift, symbol of ritual, prayer, and praising offered by the world with the assistance of the church, was presented for him by the nurse.

"Myrrh have I . . ." Its bitter perfume, the symbol of sorrow and suffering, represented the most difficult moment of the Story. The third king, a boy of 16, who, at home, had crawled on the floor all the years of his life, approached the manger in his chair, wearing a towering crown, to perform what was for him an almost impossible feat. Between his two unruly hands, incapable, ordinarily, of grasping anything, he took the precious vial containing, by his special request, real perfume.

Breathing hard, his jaws set with determination, drops of perspiration running down his face, slowly, waveringly, while everyone else stopped breathing, he managed to deliver his gift safely into the understanding hands of Mary.

The "helping" angels unhooked their crutches from the side of the manger and slowly made their way toward the Prophet who was waiting for them. Smiling, one at each of his shoulders, they again held his scroll while he read with sure voice and perfect control:

"'The people that walked in darkness have seen a great light. . . . In the beginning was the Word, and the Word was with God, and the Word was God. . . . And the Word was made flesh and dwelt among us . . . full of grace and truth. . . . And Jesus said, Except ye become as little children, ye shall not enter into the kingdom of Heaven. . . . And whoso shall receive one such little child in my name receiveth Me.'" The Prophet beckoned the people to stand. "Arise, shine, for thy light is come!" he said, his eyes flashing with authority. Then his "helping" angels closed the scroll, turned his chair, and wheeled him toward the manger that he, too, might see and adore.

Not a word was spoken by the audience. Quietly, they went forward, one by one. In true humility each stood for a moment before the manger, then turned and walked thoughtfully away—down the long corridor toward the front door, and the cold, and the darkness outside. They brought no gifts, these 200 people. Little smiles and tears were all they brought to Bethlehem that day: for unto them the gift had been given. Within them the longing child had found what he sought.

---

*From "Words From an Old Spanish Carol" in *The Long Christmas* by Ruth Sawyer (Viking).

When Tad Remembered

Minnie Leona Upton

This story dates back about 100 years to a time when diseases such a diphtheria, typhoid, scarlet fever, cholera, tuberculosis, and influenza wiped out entire families, there being no known antidote. When you add in death because of childbirth complications, you were lucky if half your children survived to adulthood. It was a mighty tough and heart-breaking time in which to live.

I have loved this old story ever since I first heard it, growing up. I have never been able to find anything about the author. In fact, this is the only one of Minnie Upton's stories I have ever found. What a pity!

I t was closing time for a little notion shop that shyly besought the scant patronage of a sleepy, shabby, old side street in a great city. The little notion shop lady sped a last lingering patron with a cheery but decided good night, then, following her outside, closed the snow-burdened blinds with tremulous haste, and, turning, peered eagerly down the length of the quiet, elm-shaded street. One long look, then the patient eyes from which the expectant light had suddenly faded, turned for a moment to the remote December stars, and a tired little sigh accompanied the clicking of the key in the lock.

Full 5,000 times had Mary Merivale done this, and nothing more interesting than Sandy MacPherson, the cobbler, putting up his shutters, or old Bettina the apple woman, ambling homeward with empty basket, had yet rewarded her searching gaze. But it was part of her day, of her life: and the warm thrill of unreasoning hope had never failed to come. Next time . . . Who could tell? Especially at Christmas time!

She hung the key on its nail and limped back into her low-ceiled sitting-room-dining room-kitchen. With resolute cheerfulness she opened the drafts and woke the slumbering fire in the shining stove, lighted the rose-shaded lamp, drew the curtains, and filled the diminutive teakettle. She was beginning to spread a white cloth on the wee round table (having removed the Dresden shepherdess, the pot of pansies, the cro-cheted doily, and the cretonne cover), when her operations were interrupted by a vigorous scratching on the door opening into the backyard.

The little lady's face broke into a welcoming smile, deepening a host of pleasant wrinkles. She drew the bolt, the door burst open, and in bounded a little rough-coated, brownish-yellow (or yellowish-brown) mongrel, yapping joyously, and springing up, albeit somewhat la-boriously and rheumatically, to bestow exuberant kisses upon the beloved hands of his lady.

"There, there, Taddy! There, there; that'll do," she said.

But there was not a marked firmness in the prohi-

41

bition, and it was several minutes before Tad subsided and sank, with asthmatic wheezes, upon a braided rug that looked as if it might have been made from Joseph's coat of many colors.

"Been watchin' for the rat, Taddy?"

Tad thumped the mat with his happy, low-bred, undocked tail. He took no shame to himself that a year's efforts had failed to catch and bring to justice the canny old rat that under the waste barrel house made carefree entrances and exits through a hole that led to regions unknown. He knew nothing of the countless times when the bold bandit had skipped nonchalantly forth while he was taking 40 winks.

Once the villain would not have escaped him so arrogantly nor, indeed, at all! But almost 20 conscientiously active years, plus asthma and rheumatism, had stolen away, bit by bit, his alertness of observation and elasticity of muscle, though not one iota of his warmth of heart and lightness of spirit.

He curled up contentedly on his rug and watched proceedings with eager interest, now and then putting out an affectionately arresting paw when his mistress whisked near him in her bustling to and fro.

Presently, his bowl of broth was set down before him on a square of blue-and-white oilcloth, and his lady sat herself down to her frugal meal. It ended with a tiny square of fruitcake for the lady (brought in by an old customer), and a lump of moist brown sugar for the dog.

"If you'd only chew it, Tad, 'pears to me you'd sense it more," observed Tad's mistress in a tone of gentle reproach.

Tad promptly assumed an expression of penitence and hopefulness fetchingly blended—penitence not from any reason of the nature of his offense, but because that tone in her voice always indicated that he had done something; hopefulness because of expectation of a small supplementary lump which he had hitherto received (he seeing no reason this night why the second lump should not continue). But tonight . . . Tonight no second lump was forthcoming.

The little woman spoke apologetically. "Tomorrow, I hope, Taddy dear, perhaps three lumps. Who knows? Business hasn't been very good this week (she had sold only seven cents' worth of "notions," and the rent was due), and I never ask for it, you know."

Tad didn't know. But he felt the lump in the dear voice. He got up stiffly and laid his common little head in her lap and looked comforting volumes with his great shining eyes. He licked the queer salty water that dropped on her hand from somewhere, and she began to smile and call him her comfort, whereat he wagged hilariously.

Presently, Mrs. Maguire, who had moved in next door, and whose red, white, and blue sign read "Washing and Scrubbing Dun Inside or Out," ran in for a friendly chat. (Neighborliness burgeons at Christmas time!)

"A foine loively little dawg, Mis' Merivale!" she commented enthusiastically, directing an approving pat at Tad's rough head. It descended on air. Tad had flopped over on one side and was lying with one paw raised appealingly, one eye alertly open, and the other tightly closed. "Was ivver the loikes av thot, now, for the way of a dawg!" exclaimed the admiring Mrs. Maguire.

But Mary Merivale had dropped on her knees beside the little performer, tears and smiles playing hide-

and-seek among her wrinkles. "It's a trick my Bobbie taught 'im when he was yet a wee-bit puppy near 20 years ago. Who's Bobbie? Why— But there, you're a newcomer in the neighborhood. Bobbie is my little boy— That is, he *was* my little boy. I— Mis' Maguire, there's something about you makes me feel you'd understand . . . Somehow my heart and my head have been full of remembering today. I— I would so like to tell you about Bobbie, and how it is that I'm alone . . . if it wouldn't tire you after your hard day's work."

"Mis' Merivale, just lit it pourr right out! It'll do the hearts of the two ov us good—you to pourr it out, an' me to take it in! I brought me Moike's sweater to darn, an' it's a good listenin' job." A big red hand gave the soft gray waves of Mary Merivale's hair a gentle pat. Then Mrs. Maguire began to rock to and fro as she threaded a huge darning needle and essayed to fill in a ragged aperture.

Mary Merivale, knitting swiftly on a sturdy red mitten, took up her story.

"Nineteen years ago last October my husband died; the kindest, best husband that ever lived. But we'd never been able to save much, havin' had eight children in the 17 years we'd been married, and all of them went with diphtheria except Bobbie. So doctor's bills and funeral expenses kept us in debt, the best we could do.

"And somehow, when John left me, I went all in a heap, and I was sick a long time, and when I got around again, I didn't seem to have any strength or courage. So when a nice old couple with money offered to adopt Bobbie and give him the best education money could pay for, I felt that I ought to let him go—I never could have done for him that way.

"He was such a bright little fellow, 7 years old, and could read right off in the Bible and the *Old Farmers' Almanac* without stoppin' to spell out hardly a word! Mr. and Mrs. Brown—that was their name—took to him from the start. They had him take their name at the very first. That did hurt somehow, though 'twas right. And kind of them. They'd just bought a fine place over in the next town to Benfield, where I'd always lived, and first I thought I'd see Bobbie often. But they didn't seem to like very well to see me come. . . . What? Oh, no, no! They were very kind, but I guess they thought it kept Bobbie too much stirred up to have Taddy and me droppin' in every little once in a while. I'd a-left Taddy with him, but Mrs. Brown didn't like dogs.

"Well, that winter they sold their new place and went away, and they fixed it so I never could find out their address—"

"The stony-hear-r-r-ted crathurs!" exploded Mrs. Maguire, sitting bolt upright, and dropping Mike's sweater. "Hiv'n'll punish—"

"Oh, no, no, Mrs. Maguire! They thought they were doing the best for Bobbie. They wanted to make a gentleman of him, and so did I. And finally I saw 'twas selfish of me to try to keep a-hold on him, when he had such a good chance to grow up different, somehow; and I stopped tryin' to trace him up.

"Well, instead of gainin' strength, I seemed to lose it after I got to work a while. I tried to give up the washin' and scrubbin' that I'd tried to do. So when I heard from my husband's cousin Mary (she used to dressmake on this street, but she went back to Benfield for her last sickness) that this little shop was for sale, with the good will and fixtures and stock, I took the bit of money that was left after the house was sold and the debts paid, and came here to the city and started for myself.

"Hard? Yes, it seemed so, for John had always stood between me and business. Still, I'm not the only one that's had to bear hard things. And I've made a livin'.

"But even so, if it hadn't been for Taddy, I don't know what I'd have done! He was a puppy then, and just as bright for a dog as Bobbie was for a boy. Bobbie taught him a lot of the regular tricks, such as other dogs do, but this one he just did was one that Bobbie himself invented. It was intended for an apology, and Taddy was to do it whenever he thought he'd been naughty.

"Well, at first after Bobbie went Taddy'd never do it except when I took him to see Bobbie. But after Bobbie went where we couldn't visit him anymore the little fellow began to do it for me whenever he saw me lookin' downhearted. The little scalawag had noticed that it made folks laugh, and so he thought 'twould answer that purpose, as well as be an apology. At least I'm pretty sure that was what was in Taddy's mind.

"But now, for a long time, he hasn't done it. Got out of the way of it when his rheumatism was bad. But this evenin' he saw I was a bit down (this raw weather is so tryin', don't you think?) and that reminded him, bless his heart!

"Haven't I ever heard anything of Bobbie? I was comin' to that. Two years ago an old Benfield neighbor who was sightseein' here in the city thought she saw Bobbie with a lot of medical students goin' into one of the new buildin's of the medical school. She said he looked just as she *knew* Bobbie'd look, grown up. And I

thought maybe 'twas here the Browns lived (Benfield's only 25 miles out), and it seemed real likely, somehow, that Bobbie'd be learnin' to be a doctor, for he was always doctorin' up sick dogs and cats and birds. I went

right out to the school, leavin' Miss Jenks, the neighbor, to tend shop. Seemed as though I couldn't get there soon enough. But no, there wasn't any Robert Brown there studyin'. All the strength went out of me. Not that I meant to thrust myself on him, and mortify him, when he'd got to be a gentleman, but I just thought I could plan to see him once in a while as he went in and out."

Mrs. Maguire made a noncommittal sound, something between a sob and a grunt.

Mary Merivale went on, unheeding. "No, I'd never thrust myself on him. But somehow—I know it's weak and selfish—but somehow, way down in my heart, I've never give up the idea that sometime Bobbie'd trace *me* out. Mis' Maguire, I've never said this to another livin' bein'. But someway, 'twould seem like Bobbie.

"He's 26 now, almost. When I go out to close the shop blind at night, I can almost *see* him comin' along the street, with his fine, big square shoulders back, and his head up! He looked so much like his father when he was little that I'm almost sure he looks *just* like him now.

"Yes, yes, Mis' Maguire, it is a true sayin'—'If it wa'n't for hope, the heart would break!' Yes, thank God for hope!

"Must you go now? Well, it *is* gettin' late—I've run on so. Yes, I *will* run in soon. Real neighborin' is such a comfort. And I can talk freer to you than I ever could to anybody else. You don't try to—to plan for me, or criticize. Just sit and listen, with your face so kind. Rather go in at your back door? Then I'll go out with you to the back gate for a bit of fresh air."

Tad politely preceded the two, as escort. But just outside the gate he caught sight of his ancient foe, the cobbler's big gray cat, and started in ardent pursuit.

"He'll soon be back!" laughed his mistress, and propped the gate ajar with a brick and left the back door open a bit as she went about her preparations for the night.

But Tad did not come back, triumphant over a routed foe, or comically disgruntled over one who had proved far too quick for him. All night his mistress lay broad awake, getting up every few minutes to go out in the alley and call, and listen. But in vain! Morning came at last, and she rose listlessly and opened the little shop, prepared her scanty breakfast, and cleared it away, untouched.

She laid the case before her paper boy, and he enthusiastically enlisted all the neighborhood boys in the search. Heart and soul, and alert eyes and nimble legs, they entered into it, for they were all loyal to Tad and his mistress, and not a boy but was glad to do the little notion shop lady a good turn. Such multitudinously active good will was an unspeakable comfort, but it did not result in Tad.

The first day dragged interminably away, then another, and another. Mary Merivale went out early on that third day to close her blinds. She could not bear to see another customer. Almost she did not look up and down the street.

"What's the use?" sighed a gray little whisper. But then her brave heart lifted itself once more. She stepped far out on the sidewalk and raised her eyes.

Round the corner of the street, bright under the last level sunshine of a perfect December day, a little shape trotted gayly in front of a stalwart figure, tall, white-clad. Then a succession—no, a tangle of joyous yaps sounded on the still air.

Mary Merivale ran forward a few unsteady steps and stopped. The athletic figure, seen in the radiant sunlight through her tears, looked like a tall, haloed angel. Strong arms closed around her, and warm kisses rained on her forehead, her lips, her cheeks, her hair!

"Motherdee!"

"Bobbie!"

Suddenly Tad stopped jumping up and trying to climb to their shoulders. They looked down through joyful tears. There he lay, an appealing paw up, one eye alertly open, and the other screwed tight shut!

"Oh, Mother, Mother; 'twas *that* that did it. Found you, I mean! Oh, Mother, I tried so hard to trace you for a while, after I got to be a big fellow in high school, and— and sensed things. But I couldn't, for the people who knew where you'd moved when you gave up the old house had died, or gone nobody knew where; and all my letters came back. And finally I was told you were dead. And the name and the age in the paper were the same."

"That was your father's cousin, Mary. But never mind now!"

"Oh, Mother! And then old Mr. Brown and his wife died suddenly. They'd looked out for me legally, you know. But the relatives were so— so fresh that I vowed I'd never take a cent of the money. And I didn't! I'd got a start, and I've worked my way. And I took back my own name, Mother—*our* name!"

"I'm so proud of you! Go on, Bobbie boy!"

"Well, I worked my way through college and medical school, and I'm to graduate this year—this school right here in the city. Mother, think! Here all these years, three years, and never found each other! How can such things be?

"And today, Mother, oh, Mother, we— we— Mother, I thought I ought to do it for the good of humanity, but I'll never have part in any such thing again. Never! I'll learn some other way! Today we were going to experiment on a dog; yes, a live dog! And everything was ready, and the dog was brought in, and, oh, I'd done such things often enough, and we were joking and laughing. But somehow there was a look in this dog's eyes that— that— well, all of a sudden I wanted to cry. And I felt myself choking up, and I stooped down and patted him. And what did the little chap do but whop over and perform that blessed old trick! Then I remembered; then I *knew!*

"And, Mother, they say medical students get callous, are a hard-hearted lot. But if you could have seen them, and the great surgeon who was to conduct the experiment (we'd had it set late, out of regular hours, to get him); if only you could have seen them, you'd have said their hearts were all right, I can tell you!

"They all came out with me, and Tad struck a bee-line for home; *home*, Mother! And I couldn't believe I'd find *you*, but I thought I'd find out *about* you and where to put the beautiful headstone I meant to buy when I got to earning money (which will be as soon as I graduate, Mother), for a fine old doctor with a big practice is going to take me in with him! And I was hurrying along when I heard a woman sing out, 'An' sure there's Mary Merivale's dawg! Praise the saints!' And then I couldn't come fast enough, and Tad couldn't, either! And then, oh, Mother, I saw you standing there with the sunshine on your dear hair, and the sweet eyes shining—the blessed, beautiful eyes that I remembered so well! And then, oh, Mother!"

"Bobbie!"

There was a silence. Then the deep young voice spoke reverently, as men speak of holy things. "And it's Christmas Eve, Mother."

The radiant eyes shone up into his.

And Tad? He dutifully began a repetition of his star act, but had his eye only half shut when he was caught up and carried into the house, his head snuggled down on a broad shoulder beside a dear, illuminated face, from which he promptly and efficiently licked the queer salty water.

Snow for Christmas

Virginia Everett Davidson

What do you do if you're the mother of two small children and too poor to buy anything? Well, perhaps you do as the Davidsons did: create paper snow!

Virginia Davidson is a freelance writer and artist in stained glass, living with her husband and two daughters in Grand Junction, Colorado.

Ginny turned on the shaking ladder and looked down. The ground wasn't so far away, but her legs wobbled worse than the framework that held her up close to the roof of the porch. Heights had affected her like this ever since the fall that knocked out three front teeth when she was 16. But she couldn't give in to fear. There was a job to do. An electric drill waited on the porch roof beside a handful of hardware, and a three-foot glass snowflake glistened in the studio upstairs, ready to be mounted on the side of the house above the porch. If only the ladder would be still!

"Need some help?" a friendly voice called from the street, where a neighbor was out walking her dog in the crisp morning.

"Oh, thanks!" Relief calmed the shakes. "I was just wishing I had someone to hold the ladder. I've made a big stained-glass snowflake to put up for the kids for Christmas. Jim'll help me hang it when he comes home from work, but right now I need to decide where's the best place to put the hooks to hold its weight."

"I'm not in a hurry; I can hold it for you."

As the ladder was steadied, Ginny climbed over the edge and onto the roof. In minutes she had analyzed the structure, marked the hook placement, and drilled the holes. The screwdriver bit replaced the drill bit, and in another minute the hooks were mounted and ready for the "big snow."

"Would you like to see the snowflake?" Ginny asked as she maneuvered the tools down the last few rungs of the ladder.

The neighbor noted where her dog was autographing trees across the street. "Sure, I can take a few minutes. He's busy."

Up in the studio, the two women stood gazing at the complex creation of silver and white. Ginny tried to imagine what it would look like outside in the sunlight. The neighbor finally voiced her thoughts. "How did you ever come up with the idea in the first place?"

"Well, it started back when the girls were little . . ." The intervening years melted like a flurry in sunshine.

* * *

Ginny was sitting with Carol and Becky at the dining table finishing up lunch. Jim, also known as Daddy, had already gone back to work. Clouds drifted in a thick, gray blanket across the usually-blue Colorado sky, and the approaching Christmas season loomed dreary and dim.

One bright spot fought against the threatening gloom—a string of miniature colored lights and a few treasured ornaments decorating a small native evergreen. Although Jim had a good job, they were still paying off student loans, and the budget was just too tight for anything more. How could she make the house cheery and Christmasy and memorable for two precious little girls with *nothing?*

Ginny stopped short. No! *Not nothing!* Back in her memory stirred a small piece of paper being skillfully folded in her mother's hands; a few artful snips, the unfolding of a snowflake. Ginny began to get excited. She knew she kept on hand a supply of the cheapest typing paper, which the girls always preferred to coloring books. She still had the good, sharp scissors her mother had given her when she went away to boarding school, and the girls had their own little scissors. In her imagination their small townhouse already danced in glorious paper snow!

"Come, Chickadee! Come, Tiddlywink! Help Mommy clear the table and clean up the kitchen, then I'll show you how to do something fun!"

The next few hours saw a growing pile of "snow" on the table, with drifts of scraps and snippets on the floor. For days every spare minute was consumed in cutting out snowflakes. Ginny had as much fun as the girls, folding and cutting, watching each snowflake emerge as it was unfolded. The process was positively addicting! The result was heaps and piles of lacy white snow. Then the intricate flakes began to appear in the windows on the front of the house, then the side, the back, even upstairs.

The favorites, the "classics," went in the kitchen window, where they could be enjoyed up close and cheer the periodic, necessary dishwashing process. And no one, but *no one,* had decorations with more Christmas spirit.

The following year the surviving snowflakes were joined in the window by a blizzard from another snowflake-cutting marathon. And another decorative dimension was added: melted onto the holey surface of an "ice candle," paper snowflakes created a gift anyone could appreciate. And oh, wouldn't a huge, grand snowflake be stunning on the outside of the house? But how to make it?

More years passed. Every December lacy paper snow decorated Jim and Ginny's windows. And every year saw the snowflakes extend to yet another realm. At one annual craft and bake sale to benefit missions, Ginny sat at a table and cut snowflakes and sold them for other people's windows. Another year the "classic" favorites were sandblasted into plate glass hexagons and sold for coasters.

After a class in stained glass, Ginny scattered a

dozen of the favorite snowflakes across a large panel in a sandblasted engraving with iridescent and frost-flower borders. It was satisfying, but still there lurked the dream of a huge white snowflake on the outside of the house at Christmas. It would look so pretty, matching the white trim, contrasting with the gray-blue clapboards. Suddenly Ginny realized what it must be. *Glass!*

It should be stained glass!

So came about the glistening snowflake Jim hung that day on the hooks over the porch. It didn't replace the lacy paper snow in the windows, but it has become a tradition in its own right. Whether or not the ground is white, Jim and Ginny and Carol and Becky always have snow for Christmas.

Anetka's Carol

Eric Philbrook Kelly

Anetka was blind. Had been since she was 3. Lightning-blind. Now, four years later as Christmas approached, her father was dumbfounded at her request. A lamp was the only present she wanted. She might not see it, but she felt sure she could feel its presence.

And so was set in motion a strange intermingling of poverty, bitter cold, sacrifice, a lamp, a comet, and a sleigh wreck—with miracles enough to go around.

One of the most beloved stories of this series is Kelly's "The Christmas Nightingale," also set in the Lublin area of Poland, which appeared in Christmas in My Heart, book 3. *My guess is that this story, too, will be gathered to the heart.*

It had been snowing for many days in the Lublin district, but on the day before Christmas the sun leaped through the clouds and shone upon a world of glittering white. It shone upon the marketplace of Lublin, where there was a very fairyland of color and happiness, of rows upon rows of Christmas booths hung with every imaginable delight—dolls and horns; beads, gold and silver glass; books with huge, pictured covers; candied statues of Saint Nikolai, the children's friend; sausages in strings; games; real leather shoes; stockings and frocks of the most fascinating colors; lanterns; candles; chocolates; wooden clocks; canes; and a million other things that drew the people from their snowbound homes and caused them, young and old, to shriek with pleasure. It shone upon the beggars in the church doors who asked for a bit of bread "for the love of the good Christ." It shone upon solemn rows of priests marching to the churches to pray for the souls of men and upon the poor children living in cellars, who held up their hands to the narrow gratings above their heads and rejoiced in the warmth. It shone upon rich churches, upon poor chapels, and upon soldiers marching in the streets, whose thoughts were of home and families far away. It shone upon the living—man, woman, and child—and upon the crosses above the graves.

Out at the edge of the Lublin forest, not 20 versts from town, it shone upon a humble peasant's cottage. The walls were only rough pine boards nailed lengthwise, and the roof, which overhung at the edges, was thick thatch. Inside the cottage, with its one living-room, a veritable turmoil existed, for five children in rough peasant dress had thrown themselves upon a man of middle age (apparently their father) and were engaged in pummeling him about (though strangely enough he seemed to be enjoying it) and shouting.

"Heigh-ho! Give over!" he was shouting. "Janek, your fingers from my throat. Stas, off my feet, you rascal, or I'll lift you out the door. Stefan, let go!" Laughing, he threw them off gently and surveyed them from a short distance while he put his clothes in order, and they, whispering eagerly, made plans for a new attack. "Order now, for I am off for town after we have eaten soup. I have a great fat pig to go in the sleigh, and

51

he must be in the market before sundown, or there'll be no Christmas tomorrow."

One, a girl of perhaps 7 years, groped toward him lovingly. He had her up in his arms in a flash and his lips to her cheek. "Anetka, my dove, what shall I get you at the Bazaar? Shall it be a doll or ribbons or sweets? Shall it be a saint on a blue box or a star all covered with paper lace? Speak and tell me what it shall be, for what you name, that I will bring."

"Boots," shouted Stas and Stefan, simultaneously. They were fat little twins, just bursting into their teens, dressed alike in yellow-gray blouses, with rough trousers thrust into the tops of shoes much too large for their feet. Their blue eyes twinkled out from be-

hind masses of hay-colored hair.

"A book," added Janek, the little man of the family who at 15 had finished his studies in the parish school.

"Ribbons!" from Marya, a year younger. She had a sweet face and dark eyes, like the mother who was dead, and her homespun clothes took nothing away from her comeliness.

Anetka, the youngest, born seven years ago in the days of war, said nothing aloud. Instead, she whispered in her father's ear.

"A lamp!" he exclaimed in surprise. "Why, what do you—" And then he stopped as tears sprang into his eyes. "Yes," he went on as he smothered some powerful feeling. "Yes, by the lightning you shall have a lamp, no matter if the twins miss their boots and Jan his book." His face was close against hers, but he drew away in order that she should not feel the moisture on his cheeks.

For Anetka, the pet and pride of Pan Kovalski, was blind. Lightning-blind, the neighbors called it, since it came with the great storm that swept the Lublin forest when the child was 3 years old. In the midst of the thunder and the roar of hail and rain, a bolt had fallen upon the oak tree that sheltered the cottage, and a ball of fire rolling down the chimney had struck down the mother and blinded the child. When they took Anetka up, they thought that nothing had happened to her, save perhaps fright and shock, but when she tried to run to her father and only fell headlong upon the floor, they knew that she could not see. The village doctor did his best for her and, in the season when crops were good, Pan Kovalski took her to the great doctor in Lublin, but his efforts were unavailing, and her blindness was not dispelled.

The Lublin doctor, however, held out some hope. "It is a curious case," he said. And while I cannot find that any part of the eyes has been destroyed or injured, yet there is some paralysis that prevents sight. This lightning bolt came as a shock. It is only possible that some shock, something unusual, may restore sight. However, the case is such a delicate one that I cannot treat it. I might harm her eyes, which in themselves seem good, and thus prevent that restoration of sight which may come at some time. And when it does come, if come it should, I think that it will be suddenly."

At this Pan Kovalski rejoiced greatly, but as the years went by and the child did not regain her sight, his hopes sank. There were times, however, when his heart was swelled with great emotion, moments in which the child would suddenly show evidences of vision, particularly in the presence of strong lights. But these evidences did not continue, and he had almost resigned himself to her blindness.

One of these occasions when her sense of vision seemed keenest came at a festival when all the neighborhood went to the parish church. The church had been in total darkness when the people entered. Pan Kovalski and Anetka were among the foremost and were sitting close to the altar rail, when suddenly a verger entered with a large lamp that he put upon a shelf above the lectern, or reader's desk. Some rays from this lamp, so different from the ordinary candles that were burned in the peasants' cottages, fell upon Anetka's eyes. She felt the gleam in some mysterious way and, though but a little child, fell upon her knees with arms outstretched, crying softly, "Light, light,

light!" It seemed to the father that a miracle had been wrought, and later when Anetka appeared to feel the same emotion as she gazed toward the reddened west at sunset time, he thought that deliverance was at hand. That sense of light was, however, the nearest she had ever come to vision, and hope at length died again.

It was no easy resolution that he took now in promising his child the lamp. Money was very scarce since the war, and taxes, high. Candles cost enough, even when purchased from the stores on saints' days or on the mother's name-day, when they were lighted at the shrine of Saint Elizabeth. A lamp meant, as well, the purchase of oil and wicks, dear enough in themselves, but Anetka was his heart's favorite and seldom asked favors. Therefore, he determined to afford her this indulgence, though the other children must forego gifts on the day of the birth of our Lord.

For who could know what the word "lamp" meant to the blind child of 7 years? Who could measure the ecstasy that burst in that soul when a realization of light leaped into her darkened eyes? Of a self-effacing disposition and little inclined to ask much for herself, the impulse must have been indeed a mighty one that prompted her to demand this costly thing. For young as she was, she knew, as all peasants knew, the value of money and the difficulty of procuring it. It is light that cheers us when we are downhearted; it is light that brings us solace out of suffering; it is light that beams upon us when we discover some new, hidden truth of the universe; it is light that first greets us when we emerge into this world. To Anetka, "lamp" meant just this. And in her blindness light was the essence of her spirit's craving.

The beet soup (borsch) was soon consumed, and the horse was hitched to the sleigh. A squealing pig, well covered with blankets, was hoisted into the space beneath the driver's seat, and Pan Kovalski cracked his whip in farewell. The next moment he was off, the children running for a distance beside the horse over the thick white crust that had formed on the fallen snow, and then waved goodbye as the squeaking runners disappeared down the slope among the pines and turned into the main highway at the foot of the hill.

A goodly family. Would that the mother had lived to see it! thought Pan Kovalski as he let the horse travel swiftly along the road.

Road was scarcely the term for it, although it was the main thoroughfare between Lublin and Warsaw, for the snow had fallen so deeply that the boundaries of the road were almost lost. In light snow it was easy to travel because of the tree stumps that lined the way. This was the common method of marking highways in the country districts, where posts and railings were expensive. The tree stumps were piled along the sides, their jagged roots sticking in the air, interlocked by the same protuberances.

At Lublin he found himself, late in the afternoon, in the midst of great excitement. Everywhere on the square in front of the church were forests of Christmas trees brought in for sale. Booths that sold toys, candies, and foods were surrounded by crowds of men, women, and children, and the store windows were heaped high with dazzling wares that would tempt even a saint. Over all the din of the purchasers, the blowing of horns and the ringing of bells, could be heard the cries of the booth-keepers with their "What do you need?" "What do you need?" Crowds of boys and carolers were making ready to set out at the appearance of the first star with their little theaters, or "Szopkas," in which they manipulated puppets that depicted scenes, enacting the dramatic events of more than 1,900 years ago when Christ was born. The leaders carried stars set on poles, and behind them came the singers with a dozen carols ready for the performance and, at the last, the boy carrying the little theater with the puppet dolls. Many a heart they were to gladden that night, and many a feast they were to be invited to, for every good Christian leaves a vacant place at his table during the feasting of Christmas Eve in case the Christ Child should come along hungry. Any one who knocked at the door was to be taken in and fed, for was it not said "Inasmuch as ye have done it to the least of these, my brethren, ye have done it unto Me"?

The pig was sold at dusk, and at a good price too, for folk are generous on Christmas Eve. Pan Kovalski then went to a little inn, where travelers found warmth and comfort, to have a bite of food and something hot to drink. The man who let him in at the door said "Merry Christmas," and the man who served him his food said "Merry Christmas," and a party of strangers who entered all said "Merry Christmas." There was that in their eyes that betokened deep sincerity too, for men become, in this, children again upon the eve of Christ's birth, and remember all those things that are dearest to the heart of the world.

Pan Kovalski rejoiced as he ate. By his side lay some bundles, hurriedly done up with paper, though not with string, for string is scarce in these days since the war. In one were four pairs of high boots, as well made as the

cobbler could nail and sew them together. In another was a book, the story of *Pan Michael*, who was the glory of Polish knighthood. And in still another was a veritable paradise of colored ribbons that might have made a queen red with jealousy for their possession.

Suddenly he raised his eyes from his food. Two men in another corner of the inn were talking earnestly about something that one had read in the paper.

"Have you seen the comet?" asked one of them.

"No," answered the other. "The nights till now have been cloudy."

"There is one, however," went on the first. "I have been reading of it here. The sky will be clear this night, and we can see it. To the east it lies, not far from the center of heaven."

A comet, thought Pan Kovalski. *Then I will see it too, on my way home. The man speaks the truth; it has been cloudy weather with a vengeance. And when I reach home early in the morning I will awaken those angels of mine from their beds, and we will see this thing.*

He finished, and went out to buy Anetka's lamp. He had saved this purchase until last because he wished to buy it at one of the stores and not at one of the booths where the goods were of cheaper make. The high price that he had got for the pig had enabled him to buy all the other presents the children had wanted, after the necessary supplies were paid for, and yet leave him enough for a lamp. Or so he thought. He still had four zloties in his wallet (about eighty cents) and believed that this princely sum of money would buy the best lamp ever made.

This lamp he saw in a window. It had a body of brass with figures of men and women and trees and animals upon it, and a high top and a shade of handsome red. He pulled open the store door and entered.

"Merry Christmas, sir," said a girl who tended the counter.

"Merry Christmas, my lady," he answered, drawing off his fur cap.

"What can I get you?"

"A lamp," he answered.

She took the bright thing from the window. "It is just six zloties," she announced.

"Six zloties." The spirit of Christmas left his heart for a single second. "I have only four," he told her.

She looked at him. "Perhaps it is a gift?" she asked, not unkindly.

"It is."

"We paid four and a half zloties for it ourselves. I could hardly sell it for less than five."

"I have only four zloties." He took them with trembling fingers from his wallet.

She looked at him with a strange emotion. The nearness of Christmas had its hold upon her, too. She looked for a moment at her own plain dress and hard hands. Hers, too, was a family of little wealth; the father had died in the war.

"I want it for my daughter who is blind."

"Blind— A lamp?"

"Yes. She can feel the light."

Some boys went by outside. They were carrying a lighted szopka and singing. She heard the old words: "Lo, the King of Light." She glanced back at the man who had not moved. "Take it," she said, removing the chimney and shade and commencing to wrap it in heavy paper. "I will take four zloties." Her master, the proprietor of the store, was a hard man, but she had an extra zloty in her pocket which she meant to slip in the till after the stranger had gone.

"God bless you," said Pan Kovalski.

Her eyes were brighter than they had been for many a day when she handed him the bundle. "My greetings to the blind girl."

"I kiss your hand," he answered after the old fashion.

Out in the street again, it was crisp and cold, the air clear, and as he went for his horse and sleigh he saw the comet hanging like a great blotch of light in the eastern sky. It was a glorious thing on this holy night; people on all the streets were gazing up at it with awed eyes. Surely it betokened happiness and the coming of good times after these hard years. Did not such a star shine in the sky when our Lord was born?

Now the runners were crunching again, and the town tollgate was close at hand. They were celebrating Christmas Eve in the keeper's little hut, where a few cronies were sipping hot wine, and the man who let him through the barrier refused to take the usual penny and shouted, "Christ is born."

Exhilarating it was, on the highway. The crust was harder than it had been in the afternoon, and the runners seemed to sing in echo to the boys of the town: "Come, Shepherds, Haste to Bethlehem." The stars shone down, the trees threw black outlines on the snow, and above them all gleamed the brilliant comet, as if again out of the east had come the Child who brought peace to the earth.

Verst after verst slipped away. The horse was steaming, the bells jingling. Now and then a sleigh passed by, going toward the lights of the town, and not one driver neglected to shout a greeting, to which Pan Kovalski answered with happiness of heart.

Midnight passed. The cottage was ever nearer, but the way grew harder and harder to traverse as the distance from the town increased. Nearing the road that turned up the hill to his little dwelling, the tired horse suddenly lost the sense of direction and swung out at an angle into a field. Pan Kovalski was almost dozing at the time and did not realize that anything had happened. Then all at once his senses leaped to alertness as the sleigh floundered against the upturned roots of a tree stump that stood at the road edge just above the snow. He drew in suddenly at the reins but it was too late. The next instant the left runner was caught in the roots. The horse, frightened, tried to tear the sleigh loose, but did not succeed. There was the sound of breaking wood, the plunging forward of a frightened steed, and the sleigh careened upon its side, throwing Pan Kovalski heavily against the stump branches. He did not arise when the horse finally struggled to its feet and dashed madly across the white crust of the field, but lay crumpled on the snow with blood flowing from a cut on his forehead. Just beyond were the bundles from the town for the children, and wrenched from its paper covering by the shock of the collision was the handsome new lamp, with a red shade and an unbroken chimney beside it.

Meantime, the children had been making merry in the little cottage. Fresh pine boughs had been brought in from the forest and filled the little space with a sweet aroma. Beneath their wooden plates they put straw that night, for was not our Lord born in a bed of straw? Large chunks of wood were thrown into the brick stove until it was shiny with heat, and on its top Marya baked little cakes with sugar and spice inside.

These eaten they sat about and enjoyed themselves, thinking of the gay season that had come to all men. That they were poor and hard-working made no difference now; they knew that everywhere, in rich homes and poverty-stricken cellars, men and women and children were rejoicing with light hearts and merry faces. Marya told them the story, oft repeated, of a Christmas stag, that wonderful deer that comes out of the forest every Christmas Eve, bearing between his huge horns a little Christmas tree on which hang colored candles and shining glass and dolls and toys. Jan told of the old days in Bethlehem when all the world was cruel and at war, and a Baby was born who came to lead men to happiness and peace. It was such as they who greeted that Baby, shepherds out of the Carpathian mountains, who crossed land and sea to greet the holy Mother, and it was the poor folk that the Baby loved and tried to help. Stas and Stefan had no story, but they knew a dance worth two stories, a Cossack dance that takes all one's breath and muscle. Jan played the harmonium (accordion) while they danced, leaping, crawling, and snapping their feet together in the air.

Finally, Anetka sang. It was the carol that all Poles love and sing on Christmas Eve. They sing it in the great church in Krakow when the clock strikes twelve, and from the tower above the church trumpeters send the song away to all corners of the earth. Children,

however, sing it best. Anetka, with her childish accents, sang it through. The first verse goes something like this:

> Through night's dark shadow
> Leaps the gladsome song;
> Shepherds, acclaiming,
> Pass the news along.
> Haste, O haste thee; Christ is living,
> Bethlehem his cradle giving,
> Greet the new-born King!

They were silent for a long time after she finished, and then Jan said, "Now for sleep. Father will be back early in the morning, and we must be fresh to meet him."

The candles were extinguished, all except the one which cast its tiny light at the foot of the picture of the Christ Mother. The twins climbed up above the stove and wrestled themselves into the bed shelves. Marya climbed into her sleeping place among the pots and kettles, and Jan stretched himself out on the floor. Anetka, as the favorite, had a little town-made cot near the door. In a very few minutes all were asleep.

What dreams of light go through the heads of those who are blind? Indeed, we may not always know. But in Anetka's thoughts there blazed in dreams that night the glory of a great lamp, shedding radiance over heaven and earth. Since her father had promised her the lamp, she knew that it was already hers, and her thoughts, waking or sleeping, were of that light-spreading thing. It was in the very early morning that the thought of it burned brightest, and it seemed to come to her through her eyes. It blazed and crackled and lit up the earth about her with merry rays. All else vanished but that. The light alone was present, and in its rays she felt happy and joyous. Then suddenly it grew very cold. She awakened with a start to feel the cold air blowing upon her, for in the night the door had slipped a little from its fastening and stood open.

Yet, as she waked, she realized that the light had been more than a dream. A light—perhaps a lamp—was blazing down upon her from some distance away, she thought. She arose from the cot, fully dressed as all peasants sleep, and realized that the light came streaming in through the open door. It did not bring an instant realization that she was seeing it with her eyes; it seemed rather a part of her dream. With a cry of exultation and delight she flung herself through the open door and stood upon the thick crust that coated the snow.

Yes, there was the light shining in the heavens and off toward the east, too. A moment of doubt, and then it was plain. It was the Star of Bethlehem, shining in the sky, and it had come to her, a blind girl, to see the light which meant the birth of the Saviour of men. Never in her waking hours had she felt such a joy as that! She threw her arms above her head in the direction of the star and moved toward it down the path that led to the highway.

And as she moved, a new world came upon her. Shadowy outlines of trees grew above her toward the sky. A whiteness of snow spread itself out and increased in size with each step she took. And then she realized: *her sight was coming back!* Oh, you who have the gift of sight, do you understand what this burst of vision meant

to one who had been for four years in a pit of darkness? Do you know what the prisoner feels when he comes from his dark cell to freedom and suddenly sees the glorious world and the sun and smiling faces? If you do, then perhaps you can understand the ecstasy of this little soul, whose thoughts of light had burned so keen in the brain, that it took only a great messenger in the sky to make that thought real. Light, once released, from the soul and from the sky, leaped to make the vision secure.

Objects became clearer as she went on. She did not know where she went, nor how. She just moved in the direction of that glowing thing above, that comet that men had talked of in Lublin, that Pan Kovalski had seen from the sleigh; that comet that had come mysteriously out of a great universe and, hidden for many days by a cloud-covered sky, shone brightly above the world on the night of Christ's birth.

She turned at the highway and followed the star easily along the path beyond the fringe of trees. For some short distance the path held her steps, and then she turned again out into the fields.

At once something shone at her feet, unlike the dazzling whiteness of the snow. She took her eyes from the comet and reached down. It was metal—cold, hard, embossed—but while her untrained sight could not make it out, her fingers knew. It was a lamp. Again she stooped and took up its shade. Next came the chimney. Then, last of all, she stumbled upon a dark figure lying on the snow, moaning now, but calling in a low voice, "Jan, Marya, Anetka!"

Had her eyes given her the comprehension that she needed she would have recognized the man, but it was the voice that told her in an instant it was her father. And what could he be doing out there in the cold field? and why lying and moaning and calling her name? She knelt in the snow and put her arm under his head, calling softly, "Father, Father, Father! Do you not know me? It is I, Anetka."

He stirred, his eyes opened, and his feeble arms clasped her there, as consciousness came back to his mind. Running across the snow came Jan, for he had found the door open and had seen that Anetka's cot was empty. In a moment his strong arms had raised the fallen man from the snow. Surely, he must have frozen to death had he remained there until dawn. And in another minute all three were ascending the path to the little cottage.

The candles were lighted and the bundles collected and Pan Kovalski's head was bandaged. Then amid roars of delight the presents were passed from hand to hand, and the glorious lamp set on the table, all ready for filling. In the midst of the merriment Pan Kovalski suddenly forgot his pain, and the blood leaped to his heart in a mighty surge as Anetka came to him with shining eyes—eyes full of vision, and hope, and love—and begged him for a kiss.

"I see, I see," she cried. "I see you, Father, and I see Janek, and I see the twins. It was the star that brought me light."

In a trembling ecstasy of joy Pan Kovalski fell upon his knees, and the children with him, and on that Christmas morning no more fervent prayers of thankfulness went out from any people in the whole world than did those of rejoicing from that little cottage.

"Sing, Anetka, sing!" shouted Jan, when they had laughed and cried together and, pulling his accordion, he played the accompanying chords.

The little voice rose again in the last verse:

> *Hail Thou, whom ages*
> *Greet with us tonight;*
> *Shine through our darkness*
> *With Thy heavenly light.*
> *Prophets' hearts, and kings', were yearning*
> *For Thy Star which now is burning;*
> *Star of Bethlehem!*

The First Crèche

Arthur Gordon

Looking back into the mists of my own childhood, I remember it wasn't until I had put up our crèche, arranged the animals, shepherds, and Wise Men around the cradle and holy family that I really felt ready to welcome Christmas. But there had to be a first time. According to Christmas tradition, this is how it all started.

Christmas in My Heart readers were introduced to Arthur Gordon, former editor of Good Housekeeping, Cosmopolitan, *and* Guideposts, *in connection with his memorable story,* "The Miraculous Staircase" *in* Christmas in My Heart, 6. *If "The Legend of the First Crèche" seems familiar, quite possibly you read it when it was published in* Guideposts.

More than 700 years ago, in the village of Greccio in Italy, there lived a man who was at war with God. This was strange, because it was an age of burning faith. All over Europe great Gothic cathedrals were rising, and men were banding together to go on crusades. But to the woodcarver of Greccio, cathedrals were a mockery and crusaders were deluded men.

His name was Luigi, and he had his reasons. He was a strong man, in his early 30s, black-eyed, hot-tempered, with wonderful sensitive hands. From childhood, he had had the gift of shaping wood into marvelous imitations of life. And for a long time he accepted this talent with gratitude, as a sign of God's favor.

Indeed, for the first 30 years of his life, Luigi had been a devout man. The bas relief of the Last Supper above the church door in Greccio was his work; so was the beautiful intricate altar screen. But the day came when Luigi spat upon the ground in front of the church and brandished his fist against heaven. It was the day he learned that his daughter—his only child—was blind.

She had seemed perfect when she was born: blonde and blue-eyed like her mother, who was from Lombardy. But as the days went by, it became apparent that something was wrong. And when it was certain that the child would never see, the woodcarver of Greccio seemed to go mad.

He went no more to the little church on the hill. He refused to allow prayers in his house. He had been carving a Madonna for the Archbishop himself; he threw it into the fire. His child had been called Maria, after the mother of Jesus. He changed her name to Rosa.

His wife pleaded in vain; nothing could move him. "Go to church if you like," he told her. "Pray your useless prayers. I will have nothing to do with a God who condemns innocent children to darkness. It is better to believe in no God than in such a God as that."

In his dealings with people, he became sombre and forbidding. His voice was harsh and there was fury in his face. His work was still in demand, for his talent seemed greater than ever. But he would do secular work only.

"I have no further interest," he would say grimly, "in the so-called glory of God!"

Only with his little blind girl did he show patience and tenderness. He brought her kittens and puppies, for she loved animals. He bought her a pony and taught her to ride. The villagers grew accustomed to seeing them together—the dark-browed man and the golden-haired girl. And the child laughed often, for she was not unhappy; but the man never smiled. To an artist, blindness is like a sentence of death.

The years passed. Then in mid-December, in the year 1207, a mule train came through Greccio, carrying rich merchandise from the far corners of the earth. Among the treasures on display was a magnificent piece of ivory, thick as a man's thigh. As soon as he saw it, Luigi had the thought that he would carve it into a doll—a bambino—for his little girl. For although he no longer cared about Christmas, still it was a time for the giving of presents, and there was nothing he would not have given his afflicted child.

So with secrecy and haste he bought the ivory and took it home to his workshop. It was unfamiliar material, but the genius in Luigi's chisel was more than equal to it. In three days it was finished, the most perfect image of a newborn baby that could be imagined. Life-sized, smiling, with tiny arms outstretched, the ivory *bambino* seemed almost to breathe. Looking upon his work, Luigi knew it was good. He knew, too, that Rosa would love it, for the child had sensitive fingers like her father, and these fingers had become her eyes.

Luigi wrapped the ivory image in a cloth and put it

on a shelf. He told no one about it except his wife, and he told her only because he wanted her to make some clothes for the doll.

But even if he had let the secret of the *bambino* be known, it would have caused no great stir, for the interest of the villagers was centered elsewhere. The talk in the marketplace, on the street corners, even in the taverns revolved around just one thing: the young friar who had come to Greccio from a neighboring town to preach in the little church.

No two descriptions of this young friar were quite the same. Some people remembered only his gentle voice, others his eyes, others his pale, graceful hands. No one could say exactly what it was about his preaching, either, but people who heard him came away with an extraordinary sense of peace, of stillness, as if all the anger and bitterness and pain of living had been lifted from their hearts.

Luigi's wife heard the young friar preach, and she begged her husband to come to the church with her. Just once, she pleaded, only once. It could do no harm, could it? And it might—it just might—rekindle a spark of the faith he had once had in God.

But Luigi shook his head. "When this God of yours shows me that he can cure blindness, then I will believe in Him. But not before."

Luigi's wife bowed her head. "May I take Rosa with me to hear him, then?"

"No," said Luigi harshly. "No. And speak no more of this!"

He knew his wife would not dare to disobey him, nor did she. But she wanted desperately to bring her child into some sort of contact, however slight, with the love and warmth that seemed to flow from the young friar. And on Christmas Eve, suddenly, she thought of a way.

Luigi might never have known—he paid little attention to his wife's comings and goings. But by chance he went into his workshop and glanced at the shelf and saw that the ivory *bambino* was gone. His shout of fury brought the servants running. From a terrified maid Luigi learned that his wife had taken it to the church to have it blessed.

When an artist has created something, it is no longer merely an object; it is an extension of himself. Out into the street stalked Luigi, black anger in his heart. Up the hill he went through the pale December sunlight toward the little church, his rage steadily increasing.

But before he could reach the door, a cavalcade swept up the hill behind him. With a clatter of hooves and a spatter of mud they passed him, three young nobles, richly dressed, on foam-streaked horses, then half a dozen mounted servants, and finally two carts loaded with farm animals: sheep, goats, oxen, a donkey.

The riders pulled up at the church door with a chorus of shouts. A young man in a purple cloak took a long drink from a silver flask, tossed it to one of his companions, and sprang down from his horse.

"Francesco!" he shouted. "Francesco Bernardone! We got your message, and we are here. Where are you?"

The others dismounted and stood swaying and laughing. It seemed to Luigi that the young aristocrats were rather drunk. He came up behind one of the servants and put a heavy hand on his shoulder. "Whence come you, fellow?" he asked roughly.

The man winced under the woodcarver's grip. "From Assisi, signor."

"And who is this Francesco Bernardone that you seek here in Greccio?"

The servant pointed. "That is he—the friar."

The church door had opened, and a slender, brown-clad figure had come out. His cowl was thrown back; the late sunlight fell upon his fine-boned face.

"Welcome, my friends," he said, smiling, "and God's peace be upon you all."

The young man in the purple cloak swept his arm in a theatrical gesture. "We've brought the animals, Francisco; how much longer are you going to play this farce? Assisi isn't the same without you. The ladies miss you too!"

"I have but one lady now," the little friar said. "Her name is Poverty. That's why I had to ask you to bring the animals. I knew you wouldn't fail me."

Luigi tightened his hold on the servant's shoulder. "Who is this man?"

The servant shrugged despairingly. "In Assisi, until not long ago, he was my master's friend and drinking companion. Now, they say, he preaches the word of God. It is very strange."

Other servants were unloading the carts, where the frightened animals reared and plunged.

"A moment, please," the friar said. He walked over to the nearest cart and laid his hand on the donkey's back. "Be calm, there, Brother Ass. There is no reason to be frightened. And you, Sister Sheep, do not *baa* so pitifully. No one is going to hurt you."

He stepped back and nodded to the servants. "Lift them down gently. They will follow me, I think." And even as he spoke, the animals grew calm and still.

A hush seemed to fall upon the people, too, the riders from Assisi and the villagers who had gathered. In this sudden quiet, the friar said to the young man in the purple cloak, "Come into the church, Lorenzo. I want to show you my *praesepe*—my manger scene."

The young man said in a low voice, "I am not a true believer, Francesco. You know that."

"All the more reason for coming," the little friar said. He turned and went back into the church, and all the animals followed him, and the people too. Even Luigi followed, because he could not help it.

Inside the church, candles burned dimly and the odor of sandalwood hung in the air. Near the altar was a rude shelter made of green boughs, and in the shelter was a manger. From where he stood, Luigi could not see into the manger, but he knew what it contained, for a woman was kneeling near it, her face beautiful in the candlelight. The woman was his wife, and when she saw him watching her, her face grew more beautiful still.

Without being led, without being driven, the animals grouped themselves around the manger and grew very still. Then the little friar stood up on the steps of the altar.

"I was going to read you the Christmas story from the gospel," he said. "But my *praesepe*—my nativity scene—makes me so happy, and my heart is so full, that I am going to sing it to you."

Standing there before the altar, he began to sing, and no one who heard it ever forgot the sweetness of his song. He told the ageless story of the angels and the shepherds, of the coming of the Wise Men who brought gifts to the Babe in the manger. He sang it from beginning to end, and no one moved, no one stirred.

Even the animals seemed to be listening, as if they too could understand the words. And Luigi was prepared to believe that they could, because an even greater miracle was taking place within himself. A strange peace had come upon him, and the bitterness and the anger was gone from his heart.

Nor was his the only heart that was being changed, for when at last the music melted into silence, the young man in the purple cloak moved forward. From around his neck he took a chain of gold, and he knelt down and put it beside the manger. And after him his companions came and put down gifts, one a ring, the other a jeweled dagger.

Luigi felt a touch on his arm. Looking around, he saw the little friar smiling at him.

"You wondered if God could cure blindness," the friar said. "Well, we are watching Him do it, are we not?"

Luigi did not answer, for there was a tightness in his throat. He could see the villagers crowding forward to look into the manger, and the awe and wonder in their faces as they gazed upon his handiwork. Afterward, there were those who swore that the ivory *bambino* stirred and smiled and lifted his arms to them. But this, no doubt, was the flickering candlelight.

Then the friar said, "Please thank your daughter for the loan of her Christmas present. And now you may take it back."

Luigi shook his head. "It is where it belongs. Let it stay."

The friar said, "Tomorrow is Christmas. Your little girl would be disappointed."

"No," said Luigi, "I will make her another *bambino*. I will work all night. I will carve her a whole *praesepe*, just like yours, with the manger and the animals and the Wise Men, so that Ro . . . I mean, Maria, will have Christmas at her fingertips whenever she wants it."

So Luigi went home, leaving the ivory *bambino* behind. Hand in hand with his wife, he walked back down the hill. And he worked all night with gratitude in his heart because he knew that in his house blindness had indeed been cured—not his daughter's, but his own. And the *praesepe* he carved was a wondrous thing, the most beautiful work that Luigi had ever done, and Maria kept it always.

That, so the story goes, was how the Nativity scene first came to be reenacted at Christmas time, and that was how the first Christmas carol came to be sung. The melody that Saint Francis sang that day in the small Italian town of Greccio has been lost for centuries now. But legend says that it was not so very different from the song the angels sang above the dark Galilean hills.

On Christmas Day in the Evening

Grace S. Richmond

The Fernald children were home for Christmas—all of them, with their families. But it wasn't quite like old times, for the old church was closed. Had been for some time because of town feuds.

Nan it was who came up with the idea. Of course it was expected of her, but the others followed. Well, most of them.

Of course you can read this story without having read "On Christmas Day in the Morning" (Christmas in My Heart, 4), but you really ought not to, for you will miss so much! While the two Christmas storybooks came out separately, they were later combined into one in 1926.

Grace Richmond (1866-1959), of Fredonia, New York, was known as the novelist of the family. During the first third of this century her stories and books regularly appeared in the top magazines of the nation prior to their publication in book form by Doubleday. The old preacher in the story is most likely modeled on Mrs. Richmond's own father, the Reverend Dr. Charles Smith, a Baptist minister who preached, quite regularly, on into his 90s.

I.

All the Fernald family go back to the old home for Christmas now, every year. Last Christmas was the third one that Oliver and Edson, Ralph and Guy, Carolyn and Nan were all at the familiar fireside as they used to be in the days before they were married. The wives and husbands and children go too (when other family claims can be compromised with), and not one of them, down to Carolyn's youngest baby, who was not 1 year old last Christmas, has sustained a particle of harm from the snowy journey to North Estabrook, tucked away though it is among the hills where the drifts are deep.

Taking them all together, they are quite a company. And as Father and Mother Fernald are getting rather well along in years, and such a house party means a good deal of preparation, last year their younger daughter Nan, and her husband, Sam Burnett, and their youngest son, Guy, and his wife of a year, Margaret, went up to North Estabrook two days ahead of the rest to help with the finishing labors. Sam Burnett and Guy Fernald, being busy young men all the year round, thought it great sport to get up into the country in the winter and planned for a fortnight beforehand to be able to manage this brief vacation. As for Nan and Margaret, they are always the best of friends. As for Father and Mother Fernald . . .

"I don't know but this is the best part of the party," mused John Fernald, looking from one to another of them, and then at his wife, as they sat together before the fireplace on the evening of the arrival. "It was all over so quick last year, and you were all piling back to town and to your offices in such a hurry, you boys. Now we can have a spell of quiet talk before the fun begins. That suits us to a T, eh, Mother?"

Mrs. Fernald nodded, smiling. Her hand, held fast in Guy's, rested on his knee. Nan's charming head with its modish dressing lay against her shoulder. What more could a mother ask? Across the fireplace Sam Burnett, most satisfactory of sons-in-law, and Margaret, Guy's best beloved, who had made the year one long honeymoon to him (so he declared) completed the little circle.

There was much to talk about. To begin with, there was everybody in North Estabrook to inquire after. And though North Estabrook is but a very small village, it takes time to inquire after everybody. Quite suddenly, having asked solicitously concerning a very old woman, who had nursed most of the Fernald children in their infancy and was always remembered by them with affection, it occurred to Nan to put a question that had been on her mind ever since she had come into town on the afternoon stage.

"Speaking of Aunt Eliza, Mother, makes me think of the old church. She used to talk so much about liking to hear the bell ring, right up over her head, next door. *Does* the bell ever ring, these days, or have cobwebs grown over the clapper?"

A shadow dropped upon Mrs. Fernald's bright face, but before she could speak her husband answered for her. He was more than a little deaf, but he was listening closely, and he caught the question.

"It's a miserable shame, Nancy, but that church hasn't had a door open since a year ago last July, when the trouble burst out. We haven't had a service there since. Mother and I drive over to Estabrook when we feel like getting out. But that's not often, come winter time. Being the only church building in this end of the township, it's pretty bad having it closed up. But there's the fuss. Folks can't agree what to do, and nobody dares to get a preacher here and try to start things up on their own responsibility. But we feel it; we sure do. I don't like to look at the old meeting house, going by, I declare, I don't. It looks lonesome to me. And there's where every one of you children grew up, too, sitting there in the old family pew, with your legs dangling. It's too bad; it's too bad!"

"It's barbarous!" Guy exclaimed in a tone of disgust.

"And all over nothing of any real consequence," sighed Mrs. Fernald in her gentle way. "We would have given up our ideas gladly for the sake of harmony. But there were so many who felt it necessary to fight to have their own way."

"And feel that way still, I suppose?" suggested Sam Burnett cheerfully. "There's a whole lot of that feeling-it-necessary-to-fight in the world. I've experienced it myself at times."

They talked about it for a few minutes, the younger men rather enjoying the details of the quarrel, as those may who are outside of an affair sufficiently far to see its inconsistencies and humors. But it was clearly a subject that gave pain to the older people, and Guy, perceiving this, was about to divert the talk into pleasanter channels when Nan gave a little cry. Her eyes were fixed

67

upon the fire, as if she saw there something startling.

"People! Let's open the church ourselves and have a Christmas Day service there!"

They stared at her for a moment, thinking her half dreaming. But her face was radiant with the light of an idea that was not an idle dream.

Guy began to laugh. "And expect the rival factions to come flocking peaceably in, like lambs to the fold? I think I see them!"

"Ignore the rival factions. Have a service for everybody. A real Christmas service with holly, and ropes of greens, and a star, and music and—and a sermon," she ended, a little more doubtfully.

"The sermon, by all means," quoth Sam Burnett. "Preach at 'em, when once you've caught 'em. They'll enjoy that. We all do."

"But it's really a beautiful idea," said Margaret, her young face catching the glow from Nan's. "I don't see why it couldn't be carried out."

"Of course you don't." Guy spoke decidedly. "If people were all like you, there wouldn't be any quarrels. But, unfortunately, they are not. And when I think of the Tomlinsons and the Frasers and the Hills and the Pollocks all going in at the same door for a Christmas Day service under that roof . . . Well—" He gave a soft, long whistle. "It rather strains my imagination. Not that they aren't all good people, you know. Oh, yes! If they weren't, they'd knock each other down in the street and have it over with—and a splendid thing it would be, too. But, I tell you, it strains my imagination to—"

"Let it strain it. It's a good thing to exercise the imagination now and then. That's the way changes come. I don't think the idea's such a bad one, myself." Sam Burnett spoke seriously, and Nan gave him a grateful glance. She was pretty sure of Sam's backing in most reasonable things, and a substantial backing it was to have too.

"Who would conduct such a service?" Mrs. Fernald asked thoughtfully.

"You couldn't get anybody out to church on Christmas morning," broke in Mr. Fernald, chuckling. "Every mother's daughter of 'em will be basting her Christmas turkey."

"Then have it Christmas evening. Why not? The day isn't over. Nobody knows what to do Christmas evening, except go to dances. And there's never a dance in North Estabrook. Whom can we get to lead it? Well . . ." Nan paused, thinking it out. Her eyes roamed from Sam's to her father's, and from there on around the circle, while they all waited for her to have an inspiration. Nobody else had one. Presently, as they expected (for Nan was a resourceful young person) her face lighted up again. She gazed at Margaret, smiling, and her idea seemed to communicate itself to Guy's wife. Together, they cried in one breath: "Billy!"

"Billy! Whoop-ee!" Guy threw back his head and roared with delight at the notion. "The Reverend Billy of Saint Johns coming up to North Estabrook to take charge of a Christmas evening service! Why, Billy'll be dining in purple and fine linen at the home of one of his millionaire parishioners—the Edgecombs', most likely. I think they adore him most. *Billy!* Why don't you ask the Bishop himself?"

Margaret flushed brightly. The Reverend William

Sewall was her brother. He might be the very manly and dignified young rector of a fashionable city church, but no man who answers to the name of Billy in his own family can be a really formidable personage, and he and his sister Margaret were undeniably great chums.

"Of course Billy would!" cried Margaret. "You know perfectly well he would, Guy, dear. He doesn't care a straw about millionaires' dinners. He'd rather have an evening with his newsboys' club, anytime. He has his own service Christmas morning, of course, but in the evening—He could come up on the afternoon train—He'd love to. Why, Billy's a bachelor—he's nothing in the world to keep him. I'll telephone him first thing in the morning."

From this point on there was no lack of enthusiasm. If Billy Sewall was coming to North Estabrook, as Sam Burnett remarked, it was time to get interested—and busy. They discussed everything, excitement mounting: the music, the trimming of the church, then, more prosaically, the cleaning and warming and lighting of it. Finally, the making known to North Estabrook the news of the coming event, for nothing less than an event it was sure to be to North Estabrook.

"Put a notice in the post office," advised Guy, comfortably crossing his legs and grinning at his father. "And tell Aunt Eliza and Miss Jane Pollock, and the thing is done. Sam, I think I see you spending the next two days at the top of ladders, hanging greens. I have a dim and hazy vision of you on your knees before that stove that always used to smoke when the wind was east—the one in the left corner—praying to it to quit fussing and draw. A nice, restful Christmas vacation you'll have!"

Sam Burnett looked at his wife. "She's captain," said he. "If she wants to play with the old meeting house, play she shall—so long as she doesn't ask me to preach the sermon."

"You old dear!" murmured Nan, jumping up to stand behind his chair, her two pretty arms encircling his stout neck from the rear. "You *could* preach a better sermon than lots of ministers, if you are only an upright old bank cashier."

"Doubtless, Nancy, doubtless," murmured Sam, pleasantly. "But as it will take the wisdom of a Solomon, the tact of a Paul, and the eloquence of the Almighty Himself to preach a sermon on the present occasion that will divert the Tomlinsons and the Frasers, the Hills and the Pollocks from glaring at each other across the pews, I don't think I'll apply for the job. Let Billy Sewall tackle it. There's one thing about it: if they get to fighting in the aisles, Billy'll leap down from the pulpit, roll up his sleeves, and pull the combatants apart. A virile religion is Billy's, and I rather think he's the man for the hour."

II.

Hi, there, Ol! Why not get something doing with that hammer? Don't you see the edge of that pulpit stair carpeting is all frazzled? The preacher'll catch his toes in it, and then where'll his ecclesiastical dignity be?"

The slave driver was Guy, shouting down from the top of a tall stepladder, where he was busy screwing into place the freshly cleaned oil-lamps, whose radiance was to be depended upon to illumine the ancient interior of the North Estabrook church. He addressed his eldest brother, Oliver, who, in his newness to the situation and his consequent lack of sympathy with the occasion, was proving but an indifferent worker. This may have been partly due to the influence of Oliver's wife, Marian, who, adorned in Russian sables, was sitting in one of the middle pews, doing what she could to depress the laborers. The number of these, by the way, had been reinforced by the arrival of the entire Fernald clan, come to spend Christmas.

"Your motive is undoubtedly a good one," Mrs. Oliver conceded. She spoke to Nan, busy near her, and she gazed critically about the shabby old walls, now rapidly assuming a quite different aspect as the great ropes of laurel leaves swung into place under the direction of Sam Burnett. That young man now had Edson Fernald and Charles Wetmore, Carolyn's husband, to assist him, and he was making the most of his opportunity to order about two gentlemen who had shown considerable reluctance to remove their coats, but who were now (to his satisfaction) perspiring so freely that they had some time since reached the point of casting aside still other articles of apparel. "But I shall be much surprised," Mrs. Oliver continued, "if you attain your object. Nobody can be more obstinate in their prejudice than the people of such a little place as this. You may get them out, though I doubt even that, but you are quite as likely as not to set them by the ears and simply make matters worse.

"It's Christmas," replied Nan. Her cheeks were the color of the holly berries in the great wreaths she was arranging to place on either side of the wall behind the pulpit. "They can't quarrel at Christmas—not with Billy Sewall preaching peace on earth, good will to men to them— Jessica, please hand me that wire. . . . And come and hold this wreath a minute, will you?"

"Nobody expects Marian to be on any side but the other one," consolingly whispered merry-faced Jessica, Edson's wife (lucky fellow!), as she held the wreath for Nan to affix the wire.

"What's that about Sewall?" Oliver inquired. "I hadn't heard of that. You don't mean to say Sewall's coming up for this service?"

"Of course he is. Margaret telephoned him this morning, and he said he'd never had a Christmas present equal to this one. He said it interested him a lot more than his morning service in town, and he'd be up, loaded. Isn't that fine of Billy?" Nan beamed triumphantly at her oldest brother over her holly wreath.

"That puts a different light on it." And Mr. Oliver Fernald, president of the great city bank of which Sam Burnett was cashier, got promptly down on the knees of his freshly pressed trousers and proceeded to tack the frazzled edge of the pulpit stair carpet with interest and skill. That stair carpet had been tacked by a good many people before him, but doubtless it had never been stretched into place by a man whose eyeglasses sat astride a nose of the impressive, presidential mold of this one.

"Do I understand that you mean to attempt music?" Mrs. Oliver seemed grieved at the thought. "There are several good voices in the family, of course, but you haven't had time to practice any

Christmas music together. You will have merely to sing hymns."

"Fortunately, some of the old hymns are Christmas music of the most exquisite sort," began Nan, trying hard to keep her temper (a feat that was apt to give her trouble when Marian was about). But at the moment, as if to help her, up in the old organ-loft at the back of the church, Margaret began to sing. Everybody looked up in delight, for Margaret's voice was the pride of the family, and with reason. Somebody was at the organ, the little reed organ. It proved to be Carolyn (Mrs. Charles Wetmore). For a moment the notes rose harmoniously. Then came an interval—and the organ wailed. There was a shout of protest from the top of Guy's stepladder.

"Cut it out! Cut out the steam calliope—unless you want a burlesque! That organ hasn't been tuned since the deluge—and they didn't get all the water out then."

"I won't hit that key again," called Carolyn. "Listen, you people."

"Listen! You can't help listening when a cat yowls on the back fence," retorted Guy. "Go it alone, Margaret girl."

But the next instant nobody was jeering, for Margaret's voice had never seemed sweeter than from the old choir loft.

"Over the hills of Bethlehem,
Lighted by a star,
Wise men came with offerings,
From the East afar."

It took them all, working until late on Christmas Eve, to do all that needed to be done. Once their interest was aroused, nothing short of the best possible would content them. But when, at last, Nan and Sam, lingering behind the others, promising to see that the fires were safe, stood together at the back of the church for a final survey, they felt that their work had been well worth while. All the lights were out but one on either side, and the dim interior, with its ropes and wreaths of green, fragrant with the woodsy smell that veiled the musty one inevitable in a place so long closed, seemed to have grown beautiful with a touch other than that of human hands.

"Don't you believe, Sammy, the poor old 'meeting-house' is happier tonight than it has been for a long, long while?" questioned Nan, with her tired cheek against her husband's broad shoulder.

"I think I should be," returned Sam Burnett, falling in with his wife's mood, "if after a year and a half of cold starvation somebody had suddenly warmed me and fed me and made me hold up my head again. It does look pretty well—much better than I should have thought it could when I first saw it in its barrenness. I wonder what the North Estabrook people are thinking about this, that's what I wonder. Do you suppose the Tomlinsons and the Pollocks and the rest of them have talked about anything else today?"

"Not much else." Nan smiled contentedly, then suddenly: "Oh, Sam, the presents aren't all tied up! We must hurry back. This is the first Christmas Eve I can remember when the rattling of tissue paper wasn't the chief sound in the air."

"If this thing goes off all right," mused Burnett, as he examined the stoves once more before putting out the lights, "it'll be the biggest Christmas present North

Estabrook ever had. Peace and good will— How they need it! And so do we all . . . so do we all."

III.

There go pretty near every one of the Fernalds, down to the station. Land, but there's a lot of 'em, counting the children. I suppose they're going to meet Guy's wife's brother that they've got up here to lead these Christmas doings tonight. Queer idea, it strikes me." Miss Jane Pollock, ensconced behind the thick lace curtains of her "best parlour," addressed her sister, who lay on the couch in the sitting room behind, an invalid who could seldom get out, but to whom Miss Jane was accustomed faithfully to report every particle of current news.

"I suppose they think," Miss Jane went on with asperity, "they're going to fix up the fuss in that church with their greens and their city minister preaching brotherly love. I can tell him he'll have to preach a pretty powerful sermon to reach old George Tomlinson and Asa Fraser and make 'em notice each other as they pass by. And when I see Maria Hill coming toward me with a smile on her face and her hand out, I'll know something's happened."

"I don't suppose you would feel, sister, as if you could put out your hand to her first?" said the invalid sister rather timidly from her couch.

"No, I don't," retorted Miss Jane very positively. "And I don't see how you can think it, Deborah. You know perfectly well it was Maria Hill that started the whole thing—and then talked about me as if I was the one. How that woman did talk—and talks yet! Don't

get me thinking about it. It's Christmas Day, and I want to keep my mind off such disgraceful things as church quarrels—if the Fernald family'll let me. A pretty bold thing to do, I call it—open up that church on their own responsibility and expect folks to come and forget the past. Debby, I wish you could see Oliver's wife in those furs of hers. She holds her head as high as ever—but she's the only one of 'em that does it disagreeably, I'll say that for 'em, if they *are* all city folks now. And of course she isn't a Fernald— Here comes Nancy and her husband. That girl don't look a minute older'n when she was married five years ago. My, but she's got a lot of style! I must say her skirts don't hang like any North Estabrook dressmaker can make 'em. They're walking—hurrying up—to catch the rest. Sam Burnett's a good-looking man, but he's getting a little stout."

"Jane," said the invalid sister, wistfully, "I wish I could go tonight."

"Well, I wish you could. That is, if I go. I haven't just made up my mind. I wonder if folks'll sit in their old pews. You know the Hills' is just in front of ours. But as to your going, Deborah, of course that's out of the question. I suppose I shall go. I shouldn't like to offend the Fernalds, and they do say Guy's wife's brother is worth hearing. There's to be music too."

"I wish I could go," sighed poor Deborah, under her breath. "To be able to go—and to wonder whether you will! O, Lord,"—she closed her patient eyes and whispered it—"make them all choose to go to Thy house this Christmas Day. And to thank Thee that the doors are open . . . and that they have strength to go. And help me to bear it . . . to stay home!"

IV.

The real problem is—" said the Reverend William Sewall, standing at the back of the church with his sister Margaret and Guy Fernald, her husband, and Nan and Sam Burnett (the four who had as yet no children, and so could best take time on Christmas afternoon to make the final arrangements for the evening). "The problem is, to do the right thing tonight. It would be so mighty easy to do the wrong one. Am I the only man to stand in that pulpit, and is it all up to me?" He regarded the pulpit as he spoke, richly hung with Christmas greens and seeming eagerly to invite an occupant.

"I should say," observed his brother-in-law, Guy, his face full of affection and esteem for the very admirable figure of the young man who stood before him, "that a fellow who's just pulled off the sort of service we know you had at St. John's this morning wouldn't consider this one much of a stunt."

Sewall smiled. "Somehow this strikes me as the bigger one," said he. "The wisest of my old professors used to say that the further you got into the country, the less it mattered about your clothes but the more about your sermon. I've been wondering, all the way up, if I knew enough to preach that sermon. Isn't there any minister in town, not even a visiting one?"

"Not a one. You can't get out of it, Billy Sewall, if you have got an attack of stagefright—which we don't believe."

"There *is* one minister," Nan admitted. "But I'd forgotten all about him till Father mentioned him last night. But he doesn't really count at all. He's old, very old, and infirm."

"Superannuated, they call it," added Sam Burnett. "Poor old chap. I've seen him; I met him at the post office this morning. He has a peaceful face. He's a good man. He must have been a strong one in his time."

"Had he anything to do with the church trouble?" Sewall demanded, his keen brown eyes eager.

Nan and Guy laughed.

"Old Elder Blake? Not except as he was on his knees, alone at home, praying for the fighters on both sides," was Guy's explanation. "So Father says, and nobody knows better what side people were on."

"If I can get hold of a man whose part in the quarrel was praying for both sides, I'm off to find him," said Sewall decidedly. He picked up his hat as he spoke. "Tell me where he lives, please."

"Billy!" His sister Margaret's voice was anxious. "Are you sure you'd better? Perhaps it would be kind to ask him to make a prayer. But you won't—"

"You won't ask him to preach the sermon, Billy Sewall; promise us that!" cried Guy. "An old man in his dotage!"

Sewall smiled again, starting toward the door. Somehow he did not look like the sort of fellow who could be easily swayed from an intention once he had formed it, or be forced to make promises until he was ready. "You've got me up here," said he, "now you'll have to take the consequences. Where did you say Elder Blake lives?"

And he departed. Those left behind stared at one another in dismay.

"Keep cool," advised Sam Burnett. "He wants the old man's advice, that's all. I don't blame him. He wants to understand the situation thoroughly. Nothing like putting your head into a thing before you put your foot in. It saves complications. Sewall's head's level—trust him."

V.

I can't," said a very old man whose peaceful face was now wearing a somewhat startled expression. "I can't quite believe you are serious, Mr. Sewall. The people are all expecting you—they will come out to hear you. I have not preached for"—he hesitated—"for many years. I will not say that it would not be a happiness. If I thought I were fit. But—"

"If I were half as fit," answered Sewall gently, "I should be very proud. But I'm—why, I'm barely seasoned yet. I'm liable to warp if I'm exposed to the weather. But you, with all the benefit of your long experience, you're the sort of timber that needs to be built into this strange Christmas service. I hadn't thought much about it, Mr. Blake, till I was on my way here. I accepted the invitation too readily. But when I did begin to think, I felt the need of help. I believe you can give it. It's a critical situation. You know these people, root and branch. I may say the wrong thing. You will know how to say the right one."

"If I should consent," the other man said after a silence during which, with bent white head, he studied the matter, "what would be your part? Should you attempt"—he glanced at the clerical dress of his caller—

"to carry through the service of your church?"

Sewall's face, which had been grave, relaxed. "No, Mr. Blake," said he. "It wouldn't be possible, and it wouldn't be . . . suitable. This is a community that would probably prefer any other service, and it should have its preference respected. A simple form, as nearly as possible like what it has been used to, will be best, don't you think so? I believe there is to be considerable music. I will read the story of the birth and will try to make a prayer. The rest I will leave to you."

"And Him," added the old man.

"And Him," agreed the young man reverently. Then a bright smile broke over his face, and he held out his hand. "I'm no end grateful to you, sir," he said, a certain attractive boyishness of manner suddenly coming uppermost and putting to flight the dignity that was at times a heavier weight than he could carry. "No end. Don't you remember how it used to be, when you first went into the work, and tackled a job now and then that seemed too big for you? Then you caught sight of a pair of shoulders that looked to you broader than yours, the muscles developed by years of exercise, and you were pretty thankful to shift the load on to them? You didn't want to shirk—heaven forbid!—but you just felt you didn't know enough to deal with the situation. Don't you remember?"

The old man glanced down at his own thin, bent shoulders with a gently humorous look, then at the stalwart ones that towered above him.

"You speak metaphorically, my dear lad," he said with a kindly twinkle in his faded blue eyes. He laid his left hand on the firm young arm whose hand held his own. "But I do remember— Yes, yes, I remember plainly enough. And though it seems to me now as if the strength were all with the young and vigorous in body, it may be that I should be glad of the years that have brought me experience."

"And tolerance," added William Sewall, pressing the hand, his eyes held fast by Elder Blake's.

"And love," continued the other. "Love. That's the great thing; that's the great thing. I do love this community, these dear people. They are good people at heart, only misled as to what is worth standing out for. I would see them at peace. Maybe I can speak to them. God knows I will try."

VI.

The Fernald family alone will fill the church," observed Ralph, the bachelor son of the house. He leaned out from his place at the tail of the procession to look ahead down the line, where the dark figures showed clearly against the snow. By either hand he held a child—his sister Carolyn's oldest and his brother Edson's youngest. "So it won't matter much if nobody else comes out. We're all here; 'some in rags, and some in tags, and some in velvet gowns'."

"I can discern the velvet gowns," conceded Edson from his place just in front, where his substantial figure supported his mother's frail one. "But I fail to make out any rags. Take us, by and large, and we seem to put up rather a prosperous front. I never noticed it quite so decidedly as this year."

"There's nothing at all ostentatious about the girls'

dressing, dear," said his mother's voice in his ear. "And I noticed they all put on their simplest clothes for tonight—as they should."

"Oh, yes," Edson chuckled. "That's precisely why they look so prosperous. That elegant simplicity—you should see the bills that come in for it! Jess isn't an extravagant dresser, as women go, not by a long shot. *But*"—he whistled a bar or two of ragtime—"I can see myself now, as a lad, sitting on that fence over there"—he indicated a line of rails, half buried in snow, that outlined the borders of an old apple orchard—"counting the quarters in my trousers pockets, earned by hard labor in the strawberry patch. I thought it quite a sum, but it wouldn't have bought—"

"A box of the cigars you smoke now," interjected Ralph unexpectedly from behind. "Hullo! There's the church! Jolly, but the old building looks bright, doesn't it? I didn't know oil lamps could put up such an illumination. And see the folks going in!"

"See them coming from all directions!" Nan, farther down the line, clutched Sam Burnett's arm. "Oh, I knew they'd come out; I knew they would!"

"Of course they'll come out." This was Mrs. Oliver. "Locks and bars couldn't keep a country community at home when there is anything going on. But as to the *feeling*, that is a different matter. Oliver, do take my muff. I want to take off my veil. There will be no chance once I am inside the door. Nan is walking twice as fast now as when we started. She will have us all up the aisle before—"

"Where's Billy Sewall bolting to?" Guy sent back this stage whisper from the front of the procession, to Margaret, his wife, who was walking with father Fernald, her hand on his gallant arm. (In John Fernald's day a man always offered his arm to the lady he escorted.)

"He caught sight of Mr. Blake, across the road. They're going in together," Margaret replied. "I think Mr. Blake is to have a part in the service."

"Old Ebenezer Blake? You don't say!" Father Fernald stated in astonishment. He had not been told of Sewall's visit to the aged minister. "Well, well, that is thoughtful of William Sewall. I don't suppose Elder Blake has taken part in a service in 15 years—20, maybe. He used to be a great preacher, too, in his day. I used to listen to him when I was a young man and think he could put things in about as interesting a way as any preacher I ever heard. Good man, too, he was—and is. But nobody's thought of asking him to make a prayer in public since—I don't know when. Well, well, look at the people going in! I guess we'd better be getting right along to our seats, or there won't be any left."

VII.

The organ was playing, very softly. Carolyn was a skillful manipulator of keyboards, and she had discovered that by carefully refraining from the use of certain keys (discreetly marked by postage stamps), she could produce a not unmusical effect of subdued harmony. This unquestionably added very much to the impression of a churchly atmosphere, carried out to the eye by the Christmas wreathing and twining of the heavy ropes of shining laurel leaves, and by the massing of the whole pulpit-front in the soft, dark green of hemlock boughs and holly. To the people who entered the house with vivid memories of the burning July day when words, hardly less burning, had seemed to scorch the barren walls, this lamp-lit interior, clothed with the garments of the woods and fragrant with their breath, seemed a place so different that it could hardly be the same.

But the faces were the same. The faces. And George Tomlinson did not look at Asa Fraser, though he passed him in the aisle, beard to beard. Miss Jane Pollock stared hard at the back of Mrs. Maria Hill's bonnet in the pew in front of her, but when Mrs. Hill turned about to glance up at the organ loft to discover who was there, Miss Pollock's face became adamant, and her eyes remained fixed on her folded hands until Mrs. Hill had twisted about again and there was no danger of their glances encountering. All over the church, likewise, were people who avoided seeing each other, though conscious all down their rigid backbones, that those with whom they had fallen out on that unhappy July day were present.

There was no vestry in the old meeting-house, no retiring place of any sort where the presiding minister might stay until the moment came for him to make his quiet and impressive entrance through a softly opening pulpit door. So when the Reverend William Sewall of Saint John's of the neighboring city came into the North Estabrook sanctuary, it was as his congregation had entered: through the front door and up the aisle.

There was a turning of heads to see him come, but there was a staring of eyes, indeed, when it was seen by whom he was accompanied. The erect figure of the young man, in his unexceptionable attire, walked slowly to keep pace with the feeble footsteps of the very old man in his threadbare garments of the cut of half a century ago, and the sight of the two together was one of the most strangely touching things that had ever met the eyes of the people of North Estabrook. It may be said, therefore, that from that first moment there was an unexpected and unreckoned with influence abroad in the place.

Now to the subdued notes of the organ that had been occupied with one theme, built upon with varying harmonies but ever appearing (though perhaps no ear but a trained one would have recognized it through the veil), was added the breath of voices. It was only an old Christmas carol, the music that of a German folk song, but dear to generations of Christmas singers everywhere. The North Estabrook people recognized it, yet did not recognize it. They had never heard it sung like that before.

> "Holy night! Peaceful night!
> All is dark, save the light
> Yonder where they sweet vigils keep
> O'er the Babe, who in silent sleep
> Rests in heavenly peace."

It was the presence of Margaret Sewall Fernald who had made it possible to attempt music at this service, the music that it seemed impossible to do without. Her voice was one of rare beauty, her leadership that of training. Her husband, Guy, possessed a reliable, if uncultivated, bass. Edson had sung a fair tenor in his college glee club. By the use of all her arts of persuasion Nan had provided an alto singer from the ranks of the choir that had once occupied this organ loft (the daughter of Asa Fraser). Whether the quartet thus formed would have passed muster with the choirmaster of Saint John's may have been a question, but it is certain the music they produced was so far above what the old church had ever heard before within its walls that, had the singers been a detachment from the choir celestial, those who heard them could hardly have listened with ears more charmed.

As "Holy Night" came down to him, William Sewall bent his head. But Ebenezer Blake lifted his. His dim, blue eyes looked up, up, and up, quite through the old meeting house roof, to the starry skies, where it seemed to him angels sang again. He forgot the people assembled in front of him. He forgot the responsibilities upon his shoulders, those bent shoulders that had long ago laid down such responsibilities. He saw visions. It is the old men who see visions. The young men dream dreams.

The young city rector read the Christmas Story out of the worn copy of the Scriptures that had served this pulpit almost from the beginning. He read it in the rich and cultivated voice of his training, but quite simply. Then Margaret sang to the slender accompaniment of the little organ, the same solo that a famous soprano had sung that morning at the service at Saint John's, and her brother, William, listening from the pulpit, thought she sang it better. There was the quality in Margaret's voice that reaches hearts, a quality that somehow the famous soprano's notes had lacked. And every word could be heard too, the quiet through the house was so absolute (except when Asa Fraser cleared his throat loudly in the midst of one of the singer's most beautiful notes). At the sound, Mrs. George Tomlinson gave him a glance that

ought to have annihilated him, but it did not. She could not know that, coming from Asa Fraser, the throat-clearing was a high tribute to the song.

"How silently, how silently
The wondrous gift is given!
So God imparts to human hearts
The blessing of His Heaven. . . .
O Holy Child of Bethlehem,
Descend to us, we pray;
Cast out our sin, and enter in—
Be born in us today."

Then William Sewall made a prayer. Those who had been looking to see old Elder Blake take this part in the service began to wonder if he had been asked into the pulpit simply as a courtesy. They supposed he could pray, at least. They knew he had never ceased doing it—and for them. Elder Blake had not an enemy in the village. It seemed strange that he couldn't be given some part, in spite of his extreme age. To be sure, it was many years since anybody had asked him to take part in any service whatsoever, even a funeral service—for which, as is well understood, a man retains efficiency long after he has ceased to be of use in the pulpit, no matter how devastating may be the weather. But that fact did not seem to bear upon the present situation.

A number of people, among them Miss Jane Pollock, were beginning to feel more than a little indignant about it, and so lost the most of Sewall's prayer, which was a good one, and not out of the prayer book, though there were phrases in it that suggested that source, as was quite natural. The city man meant to do it all, then. Doubtless, he thought nobody from the

78

country knew how to do more than to pronounce the benediction. Doubtless, that was to be Elder Blake's insignificant part, to pronounce the—

Miss Jane Pollock looked up quickly. She had been staring steadily at the back of Maria Hill's mink collar in front of her through the closing sentences of the prayer. But what was this? Elder Blake had risen and was coming forward. Was he going to read a hymn? But he had no book. And he had taken off his spectacles. He could see better, as was known, without his spectacles, when looking at a distance.

William Sewall's prayer was not ended. He could no longer be heard by the people, but in his seat, behind the drooping figure of the old man, he was silently asking things of the Lord as it seemed to him he had never asked anything before. Could His poor, feeble, "superannuated" old servant ever speak the message that needed to be spoken that night? William Sewall felt more than ever that he himself could not have done it. Could Ebenezer Blake?

Make him strong, O God, make him strong, requested William Sewall, fervently. Then, forgetting even a likeness to prayer book phrase, he added, with fists unconsciously tight-clenched, in the language of the athletic field, where a few years back he himself had taken part in many a hard-fought battle, *Help him to buck up!*

VIII.

They talk about it yet in North Estabrook, though it happened a year ago. Nobody knew how it was that from a frail old man with a trembling voice that, in its first sentences, the people back of the middle of the church could hardly hear, there came to stand before them a fiery messenger from the skies. But such was the miracle, for it seemed no less. The bent figure straightened, the trembling voice grew clear and strong, the dim eyes brightened, into the withered cheeks flowed color, into the whole aged personality came back, slowly but surely, the fires of youth. And once more in a public place Ebenezer Blake became the mouthpiece of the Master he served.

Peace and good will? Oh, yes! He preached it; no doubt of that. But it was no milk-and-water peace, no sugar-and-spice good will. There was flesh and blood in the message he gave them, and it was the message they needed. Even his text was not the gentle part of the Christmas prophecy; it was the militant part: "And the government shall be upon His shoulder." They were not bidden to lie down together like lambs, they were summoned to march together like lions, the lions of the Lord.

As William Sewall looked down into the faces of the people and watched the changing expressions there, he felt that the strange, strong, challenging words were going home. He saw stooping shoulders straighten, even as the preacher's had straightened; he saw heads come up, and eyes grow light. Most of all, he saw that at last the people had forgotten one another and were remembering God.

Suddenly the sermon ended. As preachers of a later day have learned the art of stopping abruptly with a striking climax, so this preacher from an earlier generation, his message delivered, ceased to speak. He left his hearers breathless. But after a moment's pause, during which the silence was a thing to be felt, the voice spoke again. It no longer rang. It sank into a low pleading, in words out of the Book, upon which the clasped, old hands rested: "Now, therefore, O our God, hear the prayer of Thy servant and his supplications, and cause Thy face to shine upon Thy sanctuary that is desolate, for the Lord's sake."

IX.

Up in the choir loft, Guy whispered to Margaret in a choked voice, "Can't we end with 'Holy Night,' again? Nothing else seems to fit, after that."

She nodded, her eyes wet. It had not been thought best to ask the congregation to sing. There was no knowing whether anybody would sing if they were asked. Now it seemed fortunate that it had been so arranged, for somehow the congregation did not look exactly as if it *could* sing. Certainly not George Tomlinson, for he had a large frog in his throat. Not Asa Fraser, for he had a furious cold in his head. Not Maria Hill, for though she hunted vigorously, high and low, for her handkerchief, she was unable to locate it, and the front of her best black silk was rapidly becoming shiny in spots, a fact calculated to upset anybody's singing. Not even Miss Jane Pollock, for though no tears bedewed her bright black eyes, there was a peculiar heaving quality in her breathing that suggested an impediment of some sort not to be readily overcome. And it may be safely said that there was not a baker's dozen of people left in the church who could have carried through the most familiar hymn without breaking down.

So the four in the organ loft sang "Holy Night" again. They could not have done a better thing. It is a holy night indeed when a messenger from heaven comes down to this world of ours, though he take the form of an old, old man with a peaceful face, but with eyes that can flash once more with a light that is not of earth; and with lips upon which, for one last mighty effort, has been laid a coal from off the altar of the great High Priest.

> "Silent night, holy night,
> Darkness flies, all is light;
> Shepherds hear the angels sing,
> 'Alleluia! hail the King!
> Jesus Christ is here!
> Jesus Christ is here!'"

X.

George Tomlinson came heavily out of his pew. He had at last succeeded in getting rid of the frog in his throat—or thought he had. It had occurred to him that perhaps he ought to go up and speak to Elder Blake, now sitting quietly in his chair with William Sewall bending over him, though he didn't know exactly what to say that would seem adequate to the occasion.

At the same moment Asa Fraser, still struggling with the cold in his head, emerged from his pew, directly opposite. The two men did not look at each other. But as they had been accustomed to allow their meeting glances to clash with the cutting quality of implacable resentment, this dropping of the eyes on the part of each might have been interpreted to register a distinct advantage toward peace.

As each stood momentarily at the opening of his pew, neither quite determined whether to turn his face pulpitward or doorward, Samuel Burnett, coming eagerly up to them from the doorward side, laid a friendly hand on either black-clad arm. Whether Sam was inspired by heaven, or only by his own strong common sense and knowledge of men, will never be known. But he had been a popular man in North Estabrook ever since he had first begun to come there to see Nancy Fernald, and both Tomlinson and Fraser heartily liked and respected him, a fact he understood and was counting on now.

"Wasn't it great, Mr. Tomlinson?" said Sam, enthusiastically. "Great, Mr. Fraser?" He looked, smiling, into first one austere face, and then the other. Then he gazed straight ahead of him, up at Elder Blake. "Going up to tell him so? So am I!" He pressed the two arms, continuing in his friendly way to retain his hold on both. "In all the years I've gone to church I've never heard preaching like that. It warmed up my heart till I thought it would burst, and it made me want to go to work."

Almost without their own volition, Tomlinson and Fraser found themselves proceeding toward the pulpit, yet Sam's hands did not seem to be exerting any force. The force came from his own vigorous personality that was one that invariably inspired confidence. If Burnett was going up to speak to the elder, it seemed only proper that they, the leading men of the church, should go too.

William Sewall, having assured himself that his venerable associate was not suffering from a more than natural exhaustion after his supreme effort, stood still by his side, looking out over the congregation. He now observed an interesting trio approaching the platform, composed of his valued friend, Samuel Burnett, his fine face alight with his purpose, and two gray-bearded men of somewhat unpromising exterior, but plainly of prominence in the church by the indefinable look of them. He watched the three climb the pulpit stairs and come up to the figure in the chair, Sam, with tact, falling behind.

"You did well, elder, you did well," said George Tomlinson, struggling to express himself and finding only this time-worn phrase. He stood awkwardly on one foot before Ebenezer Blake like an embarrassed school boy, but his tone was sincere—and a trifle husky, on account of the untimely reappearance of the frog in his throat.

Elder Blake looked up, and William Sewall thought he had never seen a sweeter smile on a human face, young or old. "You are kind to come and tell me so, George," said he. "I had thought never to preach again. It did me good."

"It did us good, sir," said Sam Burnett. He had waited an instant for Fraser to speak, but saw that the cold in the head was in the ascendancy again. "It did me so much good that I can hardly wait till I get back to town to hunt up a man I know, and tell him I think he was in the right in a little disagreement we had a good while ago. I've always been positive he was wrong. I suppose the facts in the case haven't changed"—he smiled into the dim, blue eyes—"but somehow I seem to see them differently. It doesn't look to me worth while to let them stand between us any longer."

"Ah, it's not worth while," agreed the old man

quickly. "It's not worth while for any of us to be hard on one another, no matter what the facts. Life is pretty difficult at its best—we can't afford to make it more difficult for any human soul. Go back to town and make it right with your friend, Mr. Burnett. I take it he was your friend, or you wouldn't think of him tonight."

"Was—and is!" declared Sam, with conviction. "He's got to be, whether he wants to or not. But he'll want to—I know that well enough. We've been friends from boyhood; we'd just forgotten it, that's all."

There was a little pause. The old man sat with his white head leaning against the high back of his chair, his face upturned, his eyes, with an appeal in them, resting first upon the face of Asa Fraser, then upon that of George Tomlinson. With a common impulse, William Sewall and Samuel Burnett moved aside together, turning their backs upon the three.

Asa Fraser lifted his eyes and met those of George Tomlinson. With a palpable effort (for he was a man of few words), he spoke.

"George," said he, "I guess I made a mistake, thinking as I did."

"Asey," responded Tomlinson quickly, "I guess you weren't the only one who's made a mistake." And he held out his hand.

Fraser grasped it. With his other hand he raised his handkerchief and blew his nose once more, violently—and finally. From this point the smile in his eyes usurped the place of the moisture that had bothered him so unwontedly, and put it quite to rout.

If you imagine that this little drama had escaped the attention of the departing congregation, headed the other way, you are much mistaken. The congregation was not headed the other way. From the moment when Burnett, Fraser, and Tomlinson had started toward the pulpit, the congregation, to a man, had paused and was staring directly toward them. It continued to stare, up to the moment when the handshaking took place. But then eyes turned and met other eyes. Hearts beat fast, lips trembled, feet moved. Unquestionably, something had happened to the people of North Estabrook.

Do you know how sometimes the ice goes out of a river? From shore to shore it had been frozen, cold and hard. For many months it had grown solid, deepening and thickening until it seems as if there could be no life left beneath. Then, at last, comes sunshine and rain and warmth. The huge mass looks as impenetrable as ever, but all at once, some day—crack! The first thin, dark line spreads across the surface. Then *crack, crack, crack, crack!* In every direction the ice is breaking up. Look quickly now if you would see that frozen surface, stretching seamless between shore and shore, for suddenly dark lanes of water open up and widen while you watch. And soon, incredibly soon, the river has burst its bonds and is rushing freely once more between its banks, with only the ever-diminishing blocks of melting ice upon its surface to tell the story of its long imprisonment.

Even so, on that memorable Christmas night, did the ice in the North Estabrook church break up. *Crack!* George Tomlinson and Asa Fraser, old friends but sworn foes, had shaken hands. *Crack!* Mrs. Tomlinson and Mrs. Fraser, tears running frankly down their cheeks, had followed the example of their husbands, and glad enough to do it, for their homes lay side by side, and each had had a hard time of it, getting along without the other. Miss Jane Pollock, seeing Mrs. Maria Hill's fruitless search for her handkerchief, had long since drawn out one of her own (she always carried two) and had held it in her hand, ready to offer it, if she could just get to the point. But when she saw, upon the pulpit platform, those two gripping hands, somehow she suddenly reached the point. *Crack!* With no difficulty whatever Miss Pollock slipped the handkerchief into Mrs. Hill's hand, whispering commiseratingly, "I presume you've got one somewhere, Maria, but you just can't lay your hand on it. Don't take the trouble to return it—it isn't of any value."

And Mrs. Hill, accepting the handkerchief, wiped away the unmanageable tears, and turning round answered fervently, "I guess I *will* return it, Jane, if it's only so's to come to your house again—if you'll let me in, after all I've said."

Even as they smiled, shamefacedly but happily, at each other, similar scenes were being enacted. All about them spread the breaking ice. Incredible that it should happen in a night? Not so. The forces of nature are mighty, but they are as weakness beside the spiritual forces of nature's God.

XI.

Well, Billy Sewall, have you taken your young friend home and put him to bed?"

The questioner was Ralph Fernald, sitting with the rest of the family (or those members of it who were not still attending to the wants of little children) before the fireplace, talking things over. They had been there for nearly an hour since the service, but Sewall had only just come in.

"I've taken him home," Sewall replied. "But there was no putting him to bed. I think he'll sit up till morning—too happy to sleep, the fine old man."

They had saved the big armchair for him, in the very center of the circle, but he would have none of it. He went over to a corner of the inglenook and dropped upon the floor at his sister Margaret's feet, his arm upon her knee. When somebody protested, Guy interfered in his defense.

"Let him alone," said he. "He gets enough of prominent positions. If he wants to sit on the fence and kick his heels a while, let him. He's certainly earned the right to do as he pleases tonight. By George! Talk about magnificent teamwork! If ever I saw a sacrifice play, I saw it tonight."

Sewall shook his head. "You may have seen teamwork," said he, "though Mr. Blake was the most of the team. But there was no sacrifice play on my part. It was simply a matter of passing the ball to the man who could run. I should have been down in four yards—if I ever got away at all."

John Fernald looked at his wife with a puzzled smile. "What sort o' talk is that?" he queried. Then he went on. "I suppose you boys are giving the credit to Elder Blake, who ought to have it. But I give a good deal to William Sewall, whose eyes were sharp enough to see what we've been too blind to find out—that the old man was the one who could deal with us and make us see light on our quarrel. He did make us see it! Here

I've been standing off, pluming myself on being too wise to mix up in the fuss, when I ought to have been doing my best to bring folks together. What a difference it does make, the way you see a thing!"

He looked round upon the group, scanning one stirred face after another, as the ruddy firelight illumined them. His glance finally rested on his daughter, Nan. She too sat upon the floor, on a plump red cushion, with her back against her husband's knee. Somehow Nan and Sam were never far apart at times like these. The youngest of the house of Fernald had made perhaps the happiest marriage of them all, and the knowledge of this gave her father and mother great satisfaction. The sight of the pair returning his scrutiny with bright faces gave John Fernald his next comment.

"After the preachers, I guess Nancy and Samuel deserve about the most credit," he went on. "It was the little girl's idea, and Sam stood by her, right through." He began to chuckle. "I can see Sam now, towing those two old fellows up to the pulpit. I don't believe they'd ever have got there without him. There certainly is a time when a man's hand on your arm makes it a good deal easier to go where you know you ought to go."

"It would have taken more than my hand to tow them away," said Sam Burnett, "after they found out how it felt to be friends again. Nobody could come between them now, with an axe."

"The music helped," cried Nan. "The music helped more than anything, except the sermon. Think how Margaret worked over that old organ! And Guy and Ed and Charles hung all those greens—"

"I tacked the pulpit stair carpet," put in Oliver,

gravely. "While you're assigning credit, don't forget that."

"I stoked those stoves," asserted Ralph. "That left-hand one—Christopher! I never saw a stove like that to hand out smoke in your face. But the church was warm when I got through with 'em."

"You all did wonderfully well," came Mother Fernald's proud and happy declaration.

"All but me," said a voice from the center of the group. It was a voice nobody had ever expected to hear in an acknowledgment of failure of any sort whatsoever, and all ears listened in amazement.

"I did nothing but discourage everybody," went on the voice, not quite evenly. "I believe I'm apt to do that, though I never realized it before. But when that wonderful old man was speaking, it came to me quite suddenly that the reason my husband's family doesn't like me better—is—because—because it is my nature always to see the objections to a thing, and to discourage people about it, if I can. I—want to tell you all that—I'm going to try to help, not hinder, from now on."

There was never a deeper sincerity than breathed in these astonishing words from Marian, Oliver's wife. Astonishing, because they all understood, knowing her as they did (Oliver was oldest, and had been first to marry), what a tremendous effort the little speech had cost her, a proud woman of the world, who had never seemed to care whether her husband's family loved her or not, so that they deferred to her.

For a moment they were all too surprised—and touched, for there is nothing more touching than humility where it is least expected—to speak. Then

Ralph, who sat next to Marian, brought his fist down on his knee with a thud.

"Bully for you!" said he.

Upon Marian's other side her husband's mother slipped a warm, delicate hand into hers. Nan, leaning past Sam's knee, reached up and patted her sister-in-law's lap. Everybody else smiled, in his or her most friendly way, at Oliver's wife; and Oliver himself, though he said nothing and merely continued to stare fixedly into the fire, looked as if he would be willing to tack pulpit stair carpets for a living, if it would help to bring about such results as these.

"Marian's right in calling him a 'wonderful old man.'" Guy spoke thoughtfully. "He got us all, Fernalds as well as Tomlinsons and Frasers. He hit me square between the eyes, good and hard. But I'm glad he did," he owned, with characteristic frankness.

They all sat gazing into the fire in silence for a little after that, in the musing way of those who have much to think about. And, by and by, Father Fernald pulled out his watch and scanned it by the wavering light.

"Bless my soul!" he cried. "It's close on to 12:00! "You children ought to be in bed, oughtn't they, Mother?"

There was a murmur of laughter round the group, for John Fernald was looking at his wife over his spectacles in just the quizzical way his sons and daughters well remembered.

"I suppose they ought, John," she responded, smiling at him. "But you might let them sit up a little longer—just this once."

He looked them over once more (it was the hundredth time his eyes had gone round the circle that night). It was a goodly array of manhood and womanhood for a father to look at and call his own. Even William Sewall, the brother of his son's wife, seemed to belong to him tonight. They gave him back his proud and tender glance, every one of them, and his heart was very full. As for their mother . . . But her eyes had gone down.

"Well," he said, leaning over to clasp her hand in his own, as she sat next him, "I guess maybe just this once it won't do any harm to let 'em stay up a little late. They're getting pretty big, now. And it's Christmas Night."

Kashara's Gift

Lissa Halls Johnson

What if you are poor—but didn't use to be? What if you now live on the wrong side of the high school? What if you are Black, and so bitter about the injustice of life that you are seething inside? What if, in the gift exchange, you draw the name of the richest girl in the school?

What do you do?

Lissa Halls Johnson, the mother of three children and author of a number of stories and books geared to today's teenagers, lives and writes from Antioch, California. This particular story was featured in Tyndale House's recent anthology, Christmas by the Hearth.

I couldn't believe it. The Christmas decorations were up even before the Halloween candy had been sold out. And I knew this was going to be the worst Christmas yet. Who did my parents think they were kidding? Their "Christmas trees all over the house" were, in reality, paper bags cut out in the shapes of Christmas trees and painted green. They decided "the best Christmas presents ever" would be stuff we made from whatever we could find. Oh, joy. I'm excited. Can you tell?

At school it was just as bad. The minute Thanksgiving ended kids were bringing Christmas goodies for their friends. Secret pals were going to be big this year. During the last week of school we would be required to bring something special every day for our secret pal. On the last day we were supposed to do something rather fantastic for them. I suppose it was the rich kids who thought up this lovely idea.

The geographical placement of our school has become the designating line in town between the have-lots and the have-nots. In the old books I've read, it seemed that the railroad tracks decided what kind of person you were, depending on which side you lived. In our town we don't have railroad tracks. We have a high school.

If you enter or leave school through the massive oak front doors of the school, you're cool, have money, drive your own car, and won't need a job until after you leave that nice university your parents paid to put you through.

If you enter or leave school through the back doors with peeling green paint, your clothes probably are on the worn side. If you want money you have to work at some minimum-wage job. Good luck on getting one, though, because they go first to the unskilled guys with families. Out the back doors of our school the walls are decorated with the voice of graffiti, the streets decorated with mute rundown cars, and the Saturdays decorated with yard sales no one will go to because they know the stuff is already so used, stained, and broken that there's no use left in it.

I guess what makes it worse for me is that a long time ago I used those front doors of the high school. I was in kindergarten then. Our family owned shiny bikes and great clothes and ate dinner at home only on the nights when Mom felt like cooking. Then my dad got hurt in an auto accident. His company didn't want him back because he couldn't work like he used to. My mom couldn't get a job because she had never learned a single trade. We sold everything and moved to the back side of the high school.

My old friends pretended they didn't know me. And I could hardly make any new friends because no back door kid trusts a former front door kid. Especially a *Black* front door kid. It's like you were a traitor from the start.

In English, they passed out names for secret pals. I don't know who did this stuff, because it was always rigged that front door kids got front door kids, and back door kids got back door kids. It must have been an unspoken code of law that the back door kids didn't play the secret pal game. They never exchanged so much as a piece of peppermint candy. They snickered to cover their envy and made cruel jokes about what the front door kids exchanged.

"Kashara Sanders." I kept my head down on the desk. Maybe if I ignored the teacher he'd think I'd gone home for the day.

"Kashara," he repeated. He sighed and walked around his desk and between rows five and six until he reached my desk. He stuck a piece of folded paper underneath my arm. He touched my arm, and I jerked it away. I didn't need any sympathy from a teacher.

As he read through the rest of the list, I heard various shoe sounds, shrieks of excitement, whispers, and silence, depending on who had picked up their pal's name. I suppose I would have thrown mine out without even reading it, but my biggest flaw has always been curiosity. I waited until I was out the back door and almost home before I dug the name from my jeans pocket. *Heather Claremont*. I turned the paper over, looking for another name. This had to be a joke. A total joke. Heather Claremont? Heather's family is the richest family in town. No kidding. Her dad not only owns half the land the mall is built on, but he's also the town's foremost judge. He's on his way to being superior court judge. Fairness is supposed to symbolize how he lives. But judging by his daughter, he's got a long way to go. I sat on the low cement wall surrounding some person's house and stared at the name on my paper. I couldn't get over it.

"Kashara! Who'd you get?" Tifron down sat next to me. He reached into his sock for a piece of paper like mine.

"Heather Claremont." I could tell my voice reflected shock.

Tifron tipped his head back and laughed. "No way, girl! I think someone's pulled a major trick on you."

Tifron was one of the few people who talked to me. He talked to everyone. He could even get along with a brick wall. No one was his enemy.

"Here." I shoved the paper at him. "Let me see yours."

I opened his piece of paper and wasn't surprised at the name. A back door.

"You going to do anything?" Tifron asked, stuffing his paper back into his sock.

"I don't know," I said, still shocked. "I wasn't going to." Then a small, evil smile took over. "But maybe this is a way I can really make a statement."

Touching my arm with his finger, Tifron made a

sizzling sound, then yanked his hand away as if burned. "Whoa, girl! I'd hate to be on the receiving end of your gifts."

"What's wrong with it, Tifron? I don't have the money like she does. She'll expect something I can't give her. Besides, she has everything. There's nothing I can give her that she can't get better quality or more of."

"Then give her something she can't get."

"Funny. As if we have the money to even buy her a candy bar."

"I didn't say *buy* her anything," Tifron said, his face moving into a rare serious look. "Think about it, babe." He pushed himself off the wall and sauntered down the street.

I opened the paper and stared at it once more. I didn't like what Tifron said. I used to believe in being good to people, and stuff. You know, like the Bible tells you to. It was easy when life was easy. It's easy to be nice to people when you can buy them stuff they like. It makes them smile. It's easy to be nice to people when they're nice back. And people are always nice to you when you're dressed nice and have cool clothes and perfect hair and all that. They aren't so nice when your clothes are kinda old looking because you have to buy them used and out-of-date from Goodwill.

Give her something she can't get. I snorted at the thought. What could I give her that she couldn't get?

I slid off the wall and headed home. Once there, I took a handful of pretzels for a snack, said hey to the folks, and dumped my stuff on my bed. I looked around my room, hoping for some sort of inspiration. Do I play this secret pal game or not?

I decided not to make a decision. It could wait another day.

But several days passed, and I still hadn't made a decision. Then I looked at Heather's face. What a dumb thing to do. I'm a total softy, even though I pretend to be hard. The first two days when she had reached the end of the day and got nothing from her secret pal, I could see something in her face. It was a strange emptiness. Come on! A girl like Heather couldn't possibly think of secret pal time as important, could she?

I dragged myself home, talking to myself the whole way.

You fliphead! You can't play this game by the normal rules.

And why not? I asked me.

Because it's not a normal thing. If you had gotten a back door, you could skip it. But you didn't. You got a front door, so you have to play by those rules.

I sighed, hating my own logic. I could get out of it if I really wanted. But I could not get Heather's sad face out of my mind.

The first thing I had to do was make a card. I dragged out our stack of secondhand magazines and cut out letters and phrases and pictures until I had what I wanted. I cut one panel off a paper sack and glued the message onto it. I then folded up the sack and gave it to Tifron to give to Heather.

He passed it to her at lunch when there were so many bodies around that no one could have told who actually slipped the bag onto her plate. At first she gingerly picked it up by one corner, her face scrunched into a "eeewww!" kind of look. Fortunately, the corner she chose allowed the bag panel to fall open.

"It's a threat!" shrieked Lindy, known for her exaggerations. "Someone wants to kill you!"

At that, Heather gripped the paper with both hands and opened it. Her face broke into a smile. "Wishing you all the gifts you could never buy for yourself this Christmas," the cutout words and letters said. "Hoping with you, Your Secret Pal."

"*Yes!*" Heather exclaimed, her manicured nail pointing at the photo of a gorgeous male model with too many perfect muscles to be believed. Kids started gathering around to look at the magazine cutouts of a tropical island, a bride, the moon, some stars, a picture of a sunset clustered with clouds, and the latest James Bond standing next to his latest car.

"Great idea," Tifron said, slapping me on the back. "What's next?"

I slumped against the balcony railing. "I haven't a clue."

The next day, Heather didn't cringe when a large paper bag appeared on top of her lunch tray. She eagerly looked inside. This time her face crumpled into one of disgust. She took out a loaf of bread tinged with mold. Next came a bag of crumpled, dry doughnuts (thanks to the Dumpster behind Ed's Doughnuts). If Heather were a cat, she'd be spitting and getting her claws ready. Then she took out another paper-bag panel. "Enjoy the simple things in life. Take your best friend to feed the ducks. Think about all you have been blessed with."

I held my breath, expecting her to get really mad. Instead, I watched her body go from rigid to soft and relaxed. She held the bag of bread next to her and smiled.

Tifron walked up to me. "Moldy bread? Never would have thought of it myself."

I looked down at the ground, ashamed. "It started out because I was angry about all she has. And then I thought about how, when you can buy everything you need, you forget about the simple pleasures in life." I shrugged. "I guess it was really a lesson for me to be nice."

"One more day," Tifron cruelly reminded me. "Tomorrow's the big finale. It's supposed to be a grand gift. You ain't got much that's grand."

"I know."

"Maybe you're just lookin' at the wrong end of the picture."

That got me to thinking. I kept thinking of what I *couldn't* give Heather. Or maybe I was thinking about what I couldn't get myself. If I looked at the picture honestly, I'd see the selfish person I had become. I wanted all the things money could buy. I wanted to be respected and liked because of how I dressed, what I drove, and where I lived.

"What can I give Heather?" I muttered over and over, all the way home. I tried doing some kind of mental inventory, but I couldn't find much there. I was really good in math, but she could afford any tutor she needed. I didn't have some great ability to style hair or do nails or cook or bake or do any of that kind of stuff for her.

Going through my stuff at home didn't help much either: a few favorite books . . . a sporadically-used diary . . . a couple of dead batteries . . . my stuffed dog and bunny from when I was little.

I went to bed with useless ideas rolling around in my head. I woke early, still with no answer. I took out the scissors, the glue, and some paper. I began to cut and paste, ideas popping into my head quicker than I could use them. The whole time my heart told me, *She's going to hate this. She is* really *going to hate this*.

I got to school, late and breathless. I stuffed the bag, tied with string, into Tifron's locker. I was afraid to go to lunch.

The cafeteria was *the* place for revealing secret pals. That way everyone could *ooh* and *ahh* over all the gifts. The back door kids either stayed outside where they could ignore the action, or went upstairs and stood around the balcony railing to watch.

I debated all the way to school and through every single class about where I would be. I hadn't had the guts to sign my name to the gift, so I could stand on the balcony and watch Heather's face without her knowing it was from me. Outside, I could be oblivious to the whole thing altogether. By the time my curiosity had won me over, the cafeteria had already seen many secret pal revelations. I made my way upstairs, trying to see what was going on around one table. A crowd had gathered. Kids tried to see over shoulders. All went silent, then a roar of laughter followed. Silence. Then a roar.

"What's going on?" I asked Tiana.

"I'm not sure. I think Heather got something that everyone is interested in."

I gulped. My homemade book depicted life at the school, caricatures of teachers, students, front door and back door life. Heather was the main character. I bit my bottom lip.

The laughter ceased. Heather stood up in the middle of the parting crowd. From above, it could have been a flower unfolding around her. "Who did this?" she demanded, looking at her friends.

The cafeteria noise fluttered to a silent stop.

"Who did this?" She stamped her foot, tears pouring down her face. She began to search the whole cafeteria.

From another part of the balcony, Tifron must have pointed. Not wanting to be the culprit, everyone moved away from where his finger aimed. I was frozen in place, unable to blend in with the crowd that was inching away.

Heather parted the kids before her and marched up

the stairs to the balcony. By the time she reached the top step, I was alone. "No one," she said, her voice strong yet full of tears, "no one has *ever* had the guts to give me gifts like you have this week."

"I'm sorry," I said, unable to look her in the eyes. "It's just that I knew you were expecting *something*. But I didn't have the money to get you anything."

Heather went on as though I hadn't said a thing. "This book"—she held out the page with magazine cutouts and phrases pasted all over—"is the funniest thing I've ever read. You have caught all my friends perfectly in this story. More important, you have taught me that the best gifts don't have to cost a lot of money."

Heather took my chin in her hand and pulled it up so she could look at me. She opened her mouth to say something, then hugged me. A real hug that a friend would give. Startled, I couldn't hug her back.

To this day I don't understand what happened that week. But now the doors at the high school open for everyone. There are no more front door kids or back door kids. We are all just friends.

Anniversary

Author Unknown

The little boy remembered an anniversary of an event he had never seen. But his father had. Now he was tending his father's sheep . . . and wondering.

This is a tender little story that could be true—who knows?—for so little is recorded of Christ's 33 years of life on this earth.

The little boy sat quite alone on the hilltop, his shepherd's crook across his knees, and his small, square lunch basket beside him. He made an odd, distorted shadow in the white light of the moon, for even the fringed shawl that his mother had woven of lamb's wool could not hide the ugly hump that lay between his shoulders, a burden much too heavy for so young a lad to bear.

Far below him, dotting the hillside with other irregular shadows, were the sheep. The majority of them slept, but a few wandered aimlessly up and down the slope. The little lad, however, was not watching the flock. His head was thrown back, and his wide eyes were fixed on the sky. There was an intensity in his gaze, and a strange, wistful smile played on his lips. The smile reflected, almost, the thoughts that were dancing, will-o'-wisp fashion, through his mind.

Perhaps it will happen again, he was thinking. *Perhaps, though a third of a century has gone by. Perhaps I shall be privileged to see the great star and hear the angels' voices as my father did!*

The moon, riding high in the heavens, went under a blanket of cloud. For a moment the world was dark. The little boy sighed and lowered his eyes. *It is an omen,* he breathed, *an omen! Though it is the time of anniversary, there will be no star this night. Neither will the angels sing.*

The time of anniversary. How often the little boy had listened to the story of the miracle that had taken place so long ago! The little boy's father had been a lad himself then. He had been the youngest of the shepherds on that glorious occasion, when an angel anthem sounded across the world and a star shone above the tranquil town of Bethlehem. With the other shepherds he had come to the stable of the inn. Crowding through the narrow doorway, he had seen a woman with a baby in her arms.

"But"—the little boy's father had told the story so many times that his family and the neighbors knew it word for word—"she was no ordinary woman! There was something in her face that made one think of a lighted candle. And there was a tenderness in her smile that the very cattle felt, for they drew close to her and seemed to kneel. It was not her beauty, although beauty she did possess!"

"And the baby"—the little boy always prompted his father here—"*what of the baby?*"

The father's hand habitually touched his small son's shoulder at this point. Touched it, and drew away, as if the brief contact caused him anguish.

"The baby," he said, and his voice grew hushed,

"was as unlike other infants as his mother was different from other women. He was scarce an hour old when I gazed at him, and there was a sense of wisdom—no, do not laugh!—on his brow.

"His tiny, up-curled hands seemed mighty, indeed—I do mean it!—to hold power. I found myself kneeling, as the cattle knelt, and there was the damp of tears upon my face. Though I was a lad tall for my age, I was not ashamed."

Alone on the hillside, the little boy could almost hear the sound of his father's voice in the stillness. His father's voice telling the story of the marvelous infant and of the Wise Men, following the star also, who had come to the stable. They had come bearing gifts, the fame of which traveled through all the land. Often, the little boy had heard of the gold and frankincense and myrrh. Often, he had shivered at the tale of the great but cruel king who had ordered death to all male infants. Often, he had thrilled to the saga of a worried young mother and her sober husband, who had stolen away into the land of Egypt with her child.

"Many of us thought," the little boy's father invariably finished, "that the child had been captured and slain by Herod. Until a decade passed, and we heard rumors of a youth who bore his name, and who lectured in a temple at Jerusalem to a group of learned doctors. A few years ago we heard that this same youth, grown older, had organized a band of men, that with them he was journeying from place to place, preaching and teaching and aiding the needy. And"—here the little boy's father had a habit of lowering his voice and glancing furtively around the room—"there are some who say

that he has become the Messiah, and that he does more than champion the cause of the common people. There are some who say he performs wonderful deeds—healing the deaf, the blind, and the lepers, and even raising the dead."

Once, at this point, the little boy had interrupted. "I wish that I might meet him," he had said with ill-masked eagerness. "I wish that he might take the hump from my back and make me strong and straight like other children."

With a loving finger laid against her son's lips, the little boy's mother enjoined silence. "What must be, must be," she told him. "You were born that way, my son. It is better," she appealed worriedly to her husband, "that we change the subject? There might be listeners about."

So the little boy's father ceased to reminisce and began to discuss his vineyards and the numbers of his flock and the size of his grain crop. Just in case one of Caesar's legionaries might be lingering near.

It was growing cold on the hillside. The child drew the shawl closer about his tired body and wished that he were not a shepherd. Shepherds led a lonely life. They did not fit into the bright places of the world. Rooms gaily lighted at eventide were for the men and boys who worked hard by day and earned their moments of ease; they were not for shepherds. But what else could a crippled lad do to justify his existence? What else than tend sheep? A crippled lad who could not undertake physical labor and who had no talents?

Yawning wearily, the little boy glanced at the sky. From the position of the moon, he judged it to be middle night. It was still a long while before sunrise; still

hours before someone would come to take his place, and he could limp home. And yet middle night had its compensations, for at that time he could break his fast and partake of the lunch that his mother had packed so neatly into a basket.

As he reached for the basket and opened it slowly, he was wondering what had been prepared for his refreshment. He found, to his satisfaction, a flask of goat's milk, nearly a loaf of crusty dark bread, and yellow cheese. There were dried figs, sugary with their own sweetness. And, wrapped separately, he came upon a real treat: a cake made of eggs, sifted flour with citron in it, and raisins!

He had expected the bread and the cheese and the milk. Even the figs he had expected. But the cake was a surprise. The sort of surprise that happened to break the monotony of the little boy's routine. His eyes gleamed as he surveyed it, and some of the sadness went out of him. Carefully, he set the basket down and spread on the ground beside him the square of linen in which his mother had folded the lunch. Carefully, he laid out the flask of milk, the bread, the cheese—but not the cake. He left it tucked away in the depths of the basket so that he might not be tempted to eat it first.

"It is good to be hungry," he said aloud. "Yes, and to have food!"

From somewhere just behind him a voice spoke. It was not a loud voice, and yet the music of it seemed to carry beyond the hillside. "Indeed, yes!" said the voice. "It is good to be hungry, to have food, and to—"

Startled, for he had thought he was quite alone with his thoughts and the browsing sheep, the little boy glanced back across his crooked shoulder. He saw a man standing upon the brow of the hill, silhouetted against the night sky. Ordinarily, he would have known fear, for often there were cruel robbers abroad at middle night. But somehow the sight of this man, who was tall and muscular, failed to frighten him. He did not know why, but he instinctively completed the man's unfinished sentence: "—and to share it!" he murmured, as if in a dream. "You are a stranger, sir?"

The man came closer to the child and stood looking down upon him. "No, not a stranger," he said slowly, "never a stranger. As it happens, my journey started not far from this very place. It started years before you, my lad, saw the light. I am by way of completing a circle."

Although he couldn't imagine what the man meant, the little boy made swift response. "I was about to eat my lunch," he said, indicating the square of linen on which he had arranged the contents of his basket. "One grows ravenous on the hillside. I am a shepherd, sir. I tend my father's flock, and each night my mother packs for me a simple repast. Will you be seated, you who have journeyed so long, and break bread with me? Perhaps, you will talk with me as we eat? It grows lonely on the dark hillside. I pine, at times, for companionship."

The man continued to peer down from his impressive height. His eyes held a warm glow. *It was as if a candle burned somewhere behind them*, the little boy thought, and remembered the words that his father had spoken when he described the woman in a stable. He felt so comfortable by the man's glance that he smiled up into the kindly face. The man spoke again.

"It is a strange coincidence," he said, "the fact that you are a shepherd. For I also tend my father's flock! And I also have often grown lonely waiting for the gates of dawn to open." All at once, with a lithe movement, he seated himself upon the ground. "Are you sure that you have sufficient nourishment for two? I should not like to deprive you of anything."

Gazing fascinated into the man's face, the little boy replied, "But, yes! I have a large flask of goat's milk and some yellow cheese, and nearly a loaf of bread, and 10 figs. And," for a second he hesitated, "that's a great plenty," he finished lamely. He did not mention the cake, still wrapped in the basket. For a cake, a cake made of sifted flour, eggs, citron, and raisins was a rare delicacy. And it was not a very big cake.

The man bent forward to retie the thong of a sandal. The little boy saw that the sandal was covered with dust. He tried to keep his eyes from glancing toward his lunch basket as he tore the crusty dark bread into fragments.

"Perhaps your feet are aching," he ventured as he placed the fragments in the center of the linen cloth. "This hill is hard to climb. I am close to being spent when I reach the summit of it, but I must needs sit high so that I can watch all the sheep."

"I have climbed steeper hills than this one, my lad," the man said slowly, "and know there are steeper hills to be. My feet do not ache." Abruptly he changed the subject. "How long have you been crippled?"

Had it come from an ordinary person, the little boy would have resented such a display of curiosity. From this man the question seemed a natural one, to be answered naturally. "Why," he said, "I have never been without a hump between my shoulders. I hate it, but"—he was quoting his mother—"what must be, must be! Still," his childish face was a trifle unchildish, "it is hard to go through life looking like one of the camels that the wise men rode when they came from the East with their caravans—"

The man interrupted. "What, lad," he queried, "do you know of the wise men from the East? How does it happen that you should mention them to me this night?" He bit into a piece of the crusty, dark bread. "It is very curious!"

Laughing softly, the little boy answered. "I suppose the wise men are in my mind, because this is the time of anniversary, and I have been thinking of the Baby that was born in a stable. Before you arrived, I was hoping that once again the great star might shine and that the angels might sing. In fact, I have been watching the sky rather than the sheep."

The man asked another swift question. "What," he queried, "do you know about these holy things and about the star and the song? You are so very young!"

"All Bethlehem," the little boy explained, "heard about the star and about the infant who lay in the manger because there was no room at the inn. I know, perhaps, more than the others, for my father, a child then himself, was one of the shepherds who saw the light from the heavens and heard the angel music." The little boy had taken the flask of goat's milk into his hands. "Will you share with me this cup, sir? For perhaps you thirst?"

The man took the flask from the fragile hands. His fingers were powerful and sinewy, but as gentle as a woman's. He said, "I will share the cup with you, my lad, for I do thirst."

As he watched the man drinking deeply, the little boy thought, *It must be tiring to tramp from place to place.* He said on impulse, as the stranger set down the flask, "Will you tell me, sir, of some of the towns in which you have stayed?"

The man answered, "One town is very like another, my lad, with poverty and pain rubbing elbows against wealth; with greed taking toll, all too often, of humanity. With health on one side and illness on the other. With so few gracious deeds that one can do to help the sore distressed—and a lifetime in which to do the work is so desperately short!"

In a low tone the little boy said, "Sometimes, when I was a tot, I hoped that my life might be short, but already I am 10 years old. How old, sir, are you? I feel older than my years. . . ."

The man's voice was muted as he replied, "I am more than three times your age, lad, but I, too, feel older than my years."

The little boy spoke vehemently. "You shouldn't, because you're so strong!" he exclaimed. "When is your time of birth, sir? I was born when it was spring."

The man smiled his beautiful, luminous smile. "It's odd that you should ask, dear lad," he murmured, "for this is my day of birth. You, quite unknowing, are giving me an anniversary feast—and never has a feast been more welcome. I was weary and forlorn when I came upon you."

Weary and forlorn! As he stared at the man, the little boy queried, "Have not you any people of your own?

People with whom you can make merry on your day of birth? When my birthday arrives, Mother prepares a real feast for me, and gives me gifts. This shawl I wear—have you noted it?—she wove it for my last birthday. The year before, she pressed a sheaf of bright flowers into wax. Once, when I was smaller, she made wondrous sweetmeats of honey and grain."

The man reached over and rested his hand on the little boy's knee. "I fear," he said, "that I have grown too old and large for birthday gifts. Furthermore, my loved ones are not near enough just now to make merry with me. But, who knows? Maybe there will be a gift for me at my journey's end."

The little boy's knee felt all a-tingle under the pressure of the friendly hand. He asked, "When, sir, will you come to your journey's end?"

The man did not meet the child's gaze. "Perhaps very soon!"

The little boy was worried. "You don't look happy about it. Don't you want to come to the end of your travels? Don't you want to reach home and see what gift they have in store for you?"

The man hesitated ever so slightly. "Yes," he said at last, "I want to reach home. But the gift—It may be too beautiful to bear. Or too heavy to carry." His face looked drawn in the white moonlight. "I suppose I should be getting on. You have made this birthday very sweet, my lad!"

Peeping down at the white cloth with its remnants of bread and cheese, the little boy thought, *There seems to be as much food as ever!* Looking slantwise, he contemplated the man's face, and suddenly he was swept by a burning sense of shame. He spoke impetuously, one word tumbling over the other. "You didn't enjoy your food," he said, "and you have had no true birthday feast. That, though, you have no way of guessing, is because I have been selfish and mean!" He gulped out his confession: "I have a cake in my basket—a cake that I was saving to eat alone after you left me. It is a cake of sifted flour and eggs and citron and raisins, and *I love cake*. But now," the little boy's voice quavered, "I would not enjoy it if I ate it in a solitary fashion; it would choke me! Sir, I desire to give the cake to you as my gift. Perhaps you will munch it later, when the chill of early morn has set in, and you are on the road."

The man did not speak, but his eyes were like stars, instead of candles, as he watched his small host lift the cake from the basket and display its rich goodness. It was only when the little boy extended it toward him that he broke into speech. "Ah, my lad," he said, "you have sustained me with your bread, and we have drunk deep of the same cup. So now we will share this cake which shall be, through your bounty, my birthday cake. We will apportion it evenly and deftly, and we will eat of it together, you and I. And then you shall wait for the dawn, and I will be on my way. But as I walk along the road, I shall see a little lad's face, and shall hear a little lad's voice, and shall remember a little lad's generosity."

Gravely, as if he were handling something infinitely precious, the man took the rich cake into his fingers. Carefully, he divided it so that the two sections were equal. He said, "Bless unto us this food, my Father," and the little boy was startled, because there was no one else upon the hillside. Then he said, "This is the cake of life, lad. Enjoy it to the last crumb!"

So he and the little boy ate the cake together, and the little boy thought that he had never tasted such fare. It was as if the cake's richness were the richness of life! As he licked the last crumbs from his fingers, he felt that he was gathering force and vigor and purpose. In his mind's eye, for no reason at all, he saw a picture of himself, robust and handsome and grave, striding down the road, his weakness cast from him and his chin high.

"It's like a vision!" he said, but when the man queried as to what he meant, he hung his head and was unable to answer. Indeed, he was silent so long that the man's hand came to rest lightly upon his shoulder, lightly, but oh, so firmly! There was something in the touch that made tears hang on the little boy's lashes, that wrung from him quick, vehement words.

"Oh," he cried, "do not leave me, sir! We could be such friends, you and I. Come with me to my home and dwell with my family. My mother will bake many cakes for you, and my father will share with you of his plenty. And I—You may have my bed and my waxed flowers, and even this fringed shawl that I wear. Do not journey on, sir! Stay with me, here in Bethlehem."

The man spoke. His voice was like a great bell tolling over the hill and valley. "I must go on," he said. "I must be about my father's business. I must travel toward my destiny. But I shall never leave you, my lad, for all that. Lo, I am with you always, even unto the end of the world!"

Bowing his head in his hands, covering his misted eyes, the little boy was aware of the man's firm fingers traveling up from his shoulder until they touched his hair. But now he couldn't speak, for a pulse drummed in his throat, and a strange rhythm was hammering in his ears. When he raised his head finally, the man was gone, and the hillside was empty, save for the shadows that were the sheep.

The little boy sobbed once, and sharply, with the sense of loss and impotence. He struggled to his feet. Only he didn't have to struggle, really, for there was a curious lightness about his body, and a feeling of freshness and peace, a peace that transcended the pain of parting. But it was not until he drew the fringed lamb's wool shawl tighter across his back that he realized how straight he was standing, *and how straight he would always stand.*

A Successful Calamity

A. May Holaday

The Trents were lovable, and the Trents adored company—the more the merrier. This Christmas was going to be one grand lark! How fortunate that Mother didn't mind all the extra work.

"Mother? Where are you, Mother?"

Everybody loved the topsy-turvy Trents. This was the name by which all Glendale knew them, and judging by that first hectic week of Christmas vacation, they were doing their best to live up to it. Something unexpected was always happening in this family of five, with its individual interests and separate groups of friends; but somehow it seemed never to matter, for Mother Trent was a capable manager, with stores of valuable experience gathered from years of skillful maneuvering and last-minute upsetting of her own plans. Gradually, she had become adept at "stretching" the salad to serve nine plates instead of five. She could supplement the rolls with a pan of quick biscuits, popped into the oven at the last minute, or "piece out" the roast or the dessert in any number of ingenious ways. And never were her talents along this line allowed to grow rusty from disuse.

She beamed good-naturedly now upon the merry group seated around the long table, her eyes lingering proudly upon her own three: Phyllis, with her soft brown eyes and hair of coppery gold, home from Eastham College; Karl, tall and handsome, studying law in a down-town office; Mildred, the harum-scarum youngest; Trent, a sophomore in the academy. The two guests, chums of Karl and Phyllis, had happened to be under the Trents' hospitable roof at supper time, though perhaps it wasn't a happenstance, for they loved this informal hospitality where unexpected company seemed to mean merely the addition of an extra plate. It wasn't that way in their homes.

"Oh, Mother, it's wonderful, being home again!" Phyllis exclaimed joyously. "We never have such good times at Dana Hall, do we, Vi?"

"Indeed, we don't!" agreed Viola Brown, who was a fellow student at Eastham. "Nor such biscuits either." Viola had just finished her third, with strawberry preserves as a delicious accompaniment.

"Huh! Funny you girls can't learn to cook as Mother does." Karl addressed his sisters. "She's got you beat a hundred ways. Girls nowadays can't cook anything but divinity creams."

"Isn't that just like a man—always thinking of his own comfort?" Phyllis laughed, her temper unruffled. "I can cook, can't I, Mother?"

This brought a sort of choking sound from Karl. "Yes, maybe salad dressing and cake frosting, when you don't leave it for Nora to finish," he reminded with

99

brotherly frankness. "Oh, yes, Mother, Nora wanted me to tell you she can't come back this week. Her neuralgia is worse."

Mrs. Trent's expression grew troubled as she thought of the week ahead and realized how much she had counted on the nimble fingers of Nora, the town's capable helper-by-the-day. First, there was the house party for over New Year's; Phyllis was in debt to several, and this seemed the only way to return it. Mildred was expecting a girlfriend from the city, and Karl— She came back to the present with a start as she felt her eldest jogging her elbow with the biscuit plate.

"They do hit the right spot, Mums," Karl praised. "Got any more stowed away in the kitchen?"

The telephone jangled, and Mildred, excusing herself, rushed expectantly from the table. "It was Jean," she announced in a tragic tone on her return. "Their car is still in the garage down town, and Jean was taking me tonight to the junior concert! But I told her I knew Dad would drive us over." She glanced confidently toward her father and patted his shoulder as she passed. "Won't you, Dad?"

Mr. Trent was a pleasant, quiet-voiced man, content to shine in the reflected light of the brilliance about him. "What time must you go?" He spoke hesitatingly. "Mother and I had—"

"How about Vi, Daddy—and me?" Phyllis cut in without ceremony. "We're due at the Van Fleets' at 8:30. You'll take us, won't you?"

"I suppose Fred and I will stay at home all evening, playing that game of looking at each other, eh, Fred?" Karl caught his pal's eye and gave a slow wink.

"We might take the street car." Fred offered the suggestion politely.

"Yes, and wait half an hour for a car. Nothing doing!" Karl jeered. "But if anyone knows how to send a machine in three directions at the same time, don't be bashful."

As usual, Mrs. Trent offered the solution. Karl and Fred could first take Mildred and Jean to the academy, returning later for Phyllis and Viola. Then the boys could have the car for the rest of the evening. She and father had planned— But no matter. They could go to the Blains' any evening.

Phyllis gave a deep sigh of satisfaction. "Now that everything's arranged, let's talk about the house party. Mother, don't you think we could have just one more girl? I want Elsie. Ever since we began rooming together, she's been wonderful to me, and this is the first time I've had a chance to do anything for her. She wears the most beautiful clothes—the Winchesters have just everything! You'd just adore Elsie—wouldn't she, Vi?"

"Huh!" her brother grunted. "I see myself, proper and precise and mute as a wooden Indian while Her Highness is here."

"Elsie isn't like that at all," Phyllis defended. However, she had detected signs of weakening in her mother's expression. "Mother, you're a dear! I'll write the note and mail it tonigh— There's the phone again. I'll go."

"If you'll excuse me, I must be getting dressed." Mildred always had something important to do.

"What about the dishes?" her father reminded. "Nora isn't here, remember?"

"You'll let the dishes go, won't you, Mother? Phil

and I will do them when we get home. See you later, everybody." And she rushed gayly for the stairway.

An hour later, all was quiet. But such a trail of disorder left behind! With her invitation to write, Phyllis had no time to press her dress, and wouldn't Mother just take a minute to do it? Karl opened his laundry package and found a button missing from his favorite shirt, but it wouldn't—and didn't—take Mother long to replace it. Mildred required the deft service of her favorite "maid" at intervals, while Mr. Trent fled in despair to the seclusion of the disordered kitchen to read the evening paper.

His wife found him there after the hurried goodbyes had been said. Almost too tired to speak, she handed him the scrap of paper she had found on her pincushion: "Wore your lace scarf, Mums. Knew you wouldn't care. Love and kisses, Phil."

Mr. Trent's eyes narrowed. Then he sat up with a jerk. "Margaret, this thing has got to stop! Oh, I know what you're going to say, but even if they are the best children in Glendale, they're growing more thoughtless every day. They are all keen enough to have a part in everything that comes along, but they can't do a blessed thing unless you do it with 'em! Look at this house they left! 'Leave the dishes until we come home,'" he mocked. "Mildred knew very well who would wash all these dishes. It's just cook, cook all the time—Nora gone and extras at every meal. And does the phone ever stop ringing? Mother, how long is it since we sat down to a table without some of the children's friends here?"

"Well, quite a while. But you know Phil won't be home again until spring. Let them enjoy their friends, dear. There are so many things we can't give them, but at least we always have plenty to eat."

"Yes," the head of the house agreed readily, "and no one but you knows how it gets on the table. Seems to me we do nothing in this house but eat—and answer the phone at mealtime."

"You're not planning to go on a diet, Will!" she began in a tone of mock dismay, her eyes twinkling.

"Well, not exactly, but the girls ought to do the cooking for a while and learn what 'extras' mean."

Mr. Trent fell silent for a moment, then suddenly spoke again.

"I have it! The very thing! Brother Jim's! For ever so long he's been wanting us to spend a week with him."

"But—when—"

"Right now!" Mr. Trent jerked out his watch. "Train leaves in 40 minutes. Hurry! We may have to wait for a street car."

A vision of paradise opened before Margaret Trent's tired eyes, a vision of peace and quiet and rest. Then she started up in dismay. "But, Will, I can't! Anyway, it wouldn't be the same. The children wouldn't have any of our friends dropping in on them."

"Perhaps even that might be arranged," Mr. Trent chuckled with a boyish wink.

* * *

It was nearly 11:00, and the three young Trents were returning together, Karl having driven to the academy, and then to the Van Fleets' to escort his sisters home.

"I'm too tired to move!" yawned Mildred as she stepped up on the porch.

"How about the dishes?" It was easy for Karl to remember tasks that had been assigned to others.

"They'll have to wait until morning, don't you say so, Phil?"

But Phyllis was not listening. "Seems queer. Mother always leaves a light burning until we come in." She turned the key, switched on the hall light, and stared at the disordered dining room beyond. "Do— Do you suppose Mother's sick?"

The frightened girls raced up the stairway to their mother's room. The bed, dresser top, and floor were cluttered with clothing, hats, and shoes scattered untidily about. Could this be Mother's room? There was no trace of her presence, and the two proceeded in puzzled wonder toward their own room, where Mildred's keen eyes spied the note on the pincushion:

"Dear Children:

Sorry to leave things in such a clutter, but I know you won't mind. Dad and I started in a hurry. Hope this housekeeping money will last until our return. Oh, yes, Phil, I took your silk umbrella and your new coat. I knew you wouldn't care. Our room will come in handy for the house party guests, won't it? Have a good time!

Bye in a hurry, and love,
Mother."

Karl was the first to recover. "Where?" he gasped. "Where did she say they had gone?"

"She didn't say!" Phyllis groaned tragically. "What shall we do? Nora away— The girls invited for New Year's—And me in my three-year-old coat!"

"Maybe Mother wanted to take her scarf that you are wearing right now," Mildred ventured shrewdly.

"How much money did they leave us?" Karl was getting down to practical details, as became his new position as head of the family.

"Enough, I guess. I'm not worrying over that part of it," Phyllis shrugged. "But this awful house—and the work ahead! It isn't one bit like Mother to leave us like this. Oh, if I hadn't mailed that note to Elsie this evening!"

"Telegraph her the party's off," suggested her brother hopefully.

"Indeed, I won't! That sort of thing isn't being done. We'll have to make the best of it." Phyllis's backbone stiffened. She wouldn't be a quitter at the start.

"Tomorrow's another day," Karl yawned. "I say we sleep on this problem and tackle it in broad daylight. Don't call me too early."

And at that very moment the doorbell jangled and echoed loudly through the quiet house. In the absence of his father, Karl opened the telegram, while the girls crowded close to read it.

"Will Trent,
Glendale, Calif.
Sounds great. Celia and I reach
Glendale 11:30 p.m.
Edward Moulton."

"Uncle Ed!" Mildred gasped.
"Aunt Celia, of all people!" Phyllis echoed weakly.

"Could anything be more tragic! She's never washed a dish nor cooked a meal in all her life, Mother says. Why, we may even have to serve her breakfasts in bed! Hurry, Milly, we must get Mother's room ready for them while Karl drives down to the station."

But while Karl puzzled all the way over the first two words of the telegram, he could arrive at no conclusion as to their meaning.

The following morning began with lumpy cocoa, burned toast, and underdone cereal, while something in the form of great stacks of sticky dishes and two more meals to get loomed unpleasantly in the background, spoiling the day before it had fairly begun.

Phyllis was entirely right about dainty, lovable Aunt Celia, who, though living in an adjoining town, had seldom visited the Trents. As a helper in the present emergency, she was worse than useless.

"Let me help!" she begged eagerly. "At home the servants won't allow any interference. I'll make the cocoa. Let's see, do you use a cupful of cocoa to each cup of milk?"

"Wait!" Mildred giggled. "It's only a tablespoonful to a cup. I'll make the cocoa, Aunt Celia. I've often watched Mother."

"Maybe it would be safer." Her aunt's eyes were twinkling.

At breakfast, Uncle Ed's face wore a mysterious, important air. Apparently, nothing could ruffle his good humor. "I like toast brown and, er, very well done," he remarked pleasantly, selecting the darkest piece on the plate. "If only Margaret and Will were here! Phyllis, I've often wondered how you managed such delightful hospi-

tality in this house, but now I understand. With you and Mildred to do the cooking, why, it's simple as anything."

The elder girl's cheeks flamed to a bright crimson, with Mildred's only a shade less vivid.

Toward evening the members of the house party arrived to remain over New Year's Day. And it was with mingled feelings of pleasure and dismay that Phyllis greeted the girls and explained the situation.

"Oh, Phil, what a lark!" exclaimed Elsie Winchester, her roommate. "I love kitchens, and the shining pots and pans."

"Not so lovable after you've washed great stacks of them," Phyllis said dryly. "It's just an unexpected trick of fate, but if you think you can stand it—"

Cries of "Surely!" and "Try us!" came in emphatic chorus.

Aunt Celia met them at the door, extending a soft hand in gracious welcome. She looked charming in a gown of pale gray trimmed in bands of fur. That was her one accomplishment—keeping herself sweet and attractive.

In a sort of panic Phyllis drew Mildred into the kitchen, for everything depended upon them. In half an hour they must serve a meal to satisfy nine tremendous appetites. How did Mother ever manage it? Roast to prepare, potatoes to peel . . .

"Quick, Milly! A rag!" Phyllis dropped the small paring knife with a clatter. "Two burns and a cut finger already! Oh, dear!"

"I'll call Aunt Celia," Mildred offered.

"Don't! She's more helpless than we are, and that's enough."

But it was Elsie, "the girl who had everything," who came gallantly to the rescue.

"Don't worry, Phil," she soothed. "I learned to cook when I was about 6. Just watch me wave the magic wand."

And indeed, it seemed as if she possessed that much-desired magic, for her deft fingers soon straightened out the confusion in the kitchen. She selected the proper dishes, took up the roast, made the gravy, arranged the salad plates, and kept Mildred busy with errands to the dining room, while Phyllis marveled in silence. And it was thus that Karl Trent first saw her, enveloped from top to toe in one of his mother's big aprons, a dab of flour on one rosy cheek.

"Thought Mother had come back," he whispered to his sister, who was tying a fresh cloth on her finger.

"You'd almost think so to see how wonderfully Elsie has managed," Phyllis replied enviously. "But she's going to teach me. There won't be another Aunt Celia in *this* family!"

"Huh!" Karl grunted thoughtfully. "How are the funds holding out, Phil?"

"Not so well as I expected. It's dreadful, the cost of everything, just to eat and forget about in a few minutes! If it wasn't for the two extras . . . They're not our company and were not included in the housekeeping allowance Mother left."

"Maybe Mother had the same problem," Karl suggested quietly, "when our friends have dropped in unexpectedly. I wonder if this visit was so unexpected after all. Uncle Ed won't give me any satisfaction, but—"

"Karl, have you any money?"

He turned his pockets inside out. "Not much," he confessed. "Christmas, you know, and everything. Maybe I could borrow some until pay day. Still, I've ordered a suit—"

"Don't bother. I'll use my Christmas check." Already, Phyllis had spent the check a dozen times in joyful anticipation. But *food?* That was the very last thing she would have dreamed of buying. Then the thought of her mother in her shabby brown suit, and her father in his last year's suit, pressed and mended many times, struck her with new force. Because of her parties and her friends, they had given up real necessities; and never a word of complaint. Her clear brown eyes softened. She felt a rush of affection for the shabby little home that had welcomed so many of her friends, and for the mother whose unselfish devotion she was just now realizing. And whether the folks had planned this lesson or not, it was all right. She'd meet this emergency as her mother would have met it—head up and smiling. And next time— But there wouldn't be any "next time" that would find her so helpless.

The New Year's dinner proved a decided success, thanks to Elsie's capable management; and even Karl, to whom the kitchen suddenly had become the most attractive room in the house, was pressed into willing service. Phyllis learned far more about house parties than she had ever known, and, too, there was a continued revelation in the sharp contrast between Elsie and Aunt Celia—the one capable and dependable, the other sweet and lovable, but entirely helpless, a liability rather than an asset. Phyllis accepted the challenge. The Trent family had quite enough liabilities, but from now on it could list an additional asset.

Phyllis could not resist one thrust, however, when she noted her brother's satisfied smile as, with awkward inefficiency, he served his first meal as host, under Elsie's direction.

"Nowadays, Karl, girls can't cook anything but divinity creams," she murmured with a flash of mischief in her dark eyes.

The Carols of Bethlehem Center

Frederick Hall

Little did Gertrude know that her great sacrifice would, in the end, prove no sacrifice at all—that she would receive more than she could possibly give.

This old story, close to a century old, has touched heart-strings everywhere it has gone. Frederick Hall was a well-known inspirational writer early in the twentieth century.

There might have been no church had not the Reverend James McKenzie come just when it seemed tottering to a fall. There might have been no Sunday school had not Harold Thornton tended it as carefully as he tended his own orchard. There might have been no class number four had it not been for Gertrude Windsor. But there would have been no glad tidings in one wintry heart, save for the voices with which Eddie and the two Willies and Charlie and little Phil sang the carols that morning in the snow. And they came straight from Him who gave the angels the songs of "On earth peace, good will to men."

At the end of the winter term in Gertrude's junior year the doctor had prescribed a year of rest for her, and she had come to find it with Aunt Mehitable in the quiet of Bethlehem Center. On her first Sunday she attended the little Sunday school, and at the close of service there was an official conference.

"She would be just the one if she would," said the pastor.

"It can't go on as it is," answered the superintendent. "The deacon means well, but he doesn't know boys. There wasn't *one* here today, and only Eddie last Sunday. I wish she'd be chorister too," he added. "Did you hear her sing?"

"I doubt if she would do that. I am told she nearly broke down in college and is here to rest."

"Yes, so Mr. Thompson told me. But we do need her."

"Well, I will call on her and let you know what I learn."

* * *

Gertrude hesitated; for had not the doctor said, "It is not so much college, Miss Windsor; it is church and Sunday school and Christian Endeavor and Student Volunteer, and all the rest, on top of college work, that is breaking you down, and you must stop it!"

But the wistful face of Harry, who brought their milk, decided her. And the second Sunday saw her instructing Eddie and little Phil in the quarterly temperance lesson. It was not until school was over that she learned the reason for little Phil's conscious silence. And next day, when she met him with his father on the street, she tried to atone for her former ignorance.

"Are you Phil's father?" she asked, stepping toward them.

Tim Shartow, who was believed by some to fear neither God, man, nor the devil, grew strangely embarrassed as he took her hand after a hurried inspection of his own. "Yes'm," he answered.

"I am to be his Sunday school teacher," she went on, "and of course I want to know the fathers and mothers of my boys. I hope Phil can come regularly. We are going to have some very interesting lessons."

"I guess he can come," answered his father. "It's a better place for him than on the street anyway."

This was faint praise, but well meant. Gertrude smiled her appreciation, and in that brief meeting won not only Phil's lifelong regard but, had she known it, that of his father as well, for thenceforth Tim Shartow felt that he had two friends in Bethlehem Center of whom he need not be ashamed.

His other friend was the Reverend James McKenzie. The mutual though qualified respect they felt for each other dated from their first meeting, when Mr. McKenzie had walked into the saloon and asked permission to tack up some bills advertising his revival services.

"I guess you can," the proprietor had answered, standing alertly on his guard.

The bills had been posted, and the unwonted visitor turned to the man behind the bar. They were alone together. "We should be very glad, Mr. Shartow," he said, "if you would attend some of the meetings."

"It'll be a cold day when I do," answered the saloon-keeper.

Mr. McKenzie did not reply, but Tim said, by way of explanation, "The worst enemies I've got are in that church."

A smile lighted up the pastor's earnest face. "No, Mr. Shartow," he said, "you're wrong. They don't like your business—I don't like your business—but you haven't an enemy in our church. And I want to tell you now"—his foot was upon the bar rail, and he was looking straight into the eyes of the man to whom he spoke—"that every night, as I pray that God will remove this saloon, I shall pray that he will bring you to know my Saviour. And if ever you need help that I can give, I want you to feel free to come to me. We are traveling different roads, Mr. Shartow, but we are not enemies—we are friends."

And the pastor departed, leaving Tim, the saloon-keeper, "that shook up" (to use his own phrase) that it is doubtful whether he ever entirely regained his former attitude toward "them church folks."

By Gertrude's second Sunday as teacher, the two Willies had come to test the truth of rumors that had reached them. Charlie and Harry came next, and, after Gertrude announced the midweek class meetings as a reward for full attendance, not one absence occurred for 13 weeks.

To Harold Thornton it had the look of a miracle that the class for whom no teacher could be found was as clay in the hands of the potter. There was nothing Gertrude could not do with them. They listened spellbound while she talked, took part in the responsive readings, answered questions, studied their lessons, sat wherever the superintendent wished. They even pocketed their papers without a glance at them until the session was over. And they sang with a wild abandon that was exhilarating to hear. Even Harry, who held throughout the note on which his voice first fastened, never failed to sing; and, though it added little to the harmony, it spoke volumes for the spirit of the school and the devotion to the chorister.

But if Gertrude was doing much for the boys, they were doing much for Gertrude. And in obeying her orders to rest, exercise, and grow strong, she could not have had better helpers. From the time when the first pale blossoms of the bloodroot showed beside the snow, through the seasons of violets and wild strawberries and goldenrod, to the time when the frost had spread the ground with the split shucks of the hickory nuts, the spoil of all the woodland was brought to her.

Their class meetings became long tramps, during which Gertrude told them interesting things about insects, birds, and flowers, and they told as much that was strange to her. Every one of them had became a conspirator in the plot to keep her out of doors, away from her books; hardly a day passed that she did not go somewhere with one or more of them. And as the healthy color began to show beneath the tan, as strength came back and every pulse beat brought the returning joy of life, she often felt that all her work for class number four had been repaid a hundredfold.

It was one mid-August afternoon, when the tasseled corn stood high and the thistles had begun to take wing and fly away to join the dandelions, that there came the first thoughts of the carols. Harry had to drive cows that day, but the others were with her, and as they came out through Mr. Giertz's woods and looked down upon the pasture where the sheep were feeding, little

Phil began the quaint old version of the shepherd psalm that she had taught them:

"The Lord is my shepherd;
I shall not want;
He maketh me down to lie."

And the other boys joined, singing through to the end.

It was beautiful. She had never realized that they could sing so well. Suddenly, as she listened, the plan came full-grown into her mind, and she proposed it then and there. The boys were jubilant. For a half-hour they discussed details, and then, "all seated on the ground" like those of whom they sang, she taught them the beginning of "While Shepherds Watched Their Flocks by Night."

That was the first of many open air rehearsals that transferred, when the weather grew colder, to Willie Giertz's, where there were no near neighbors to whom the portentous secret might leak out. There was not one defective voice in the class, save Harry's, and he was at first a puzzle. But that difficulty vanished when it was learned that his fondest ambition was satisfied by striking the tuning fork. Thereafter, all went smoothly with much enthusiasm and a world of mystery.

When the program was complete, they had learned by heart six songs: "While Shepherds Watched Their Flocks by Night," "Away in a Manger," "We Three Kings of Orient Are," "Hark! the Herald Angels Sing," "There Came Three Kings 'Ere Break of Day," and last—but best, because it seemed especially made for them—the song that began,

"O little town of Bethlehem,
  How still we see thee lie!
  Above thy deep and dreamless sleep
  The silent stars go by."

And so at length came Christmas Eve. Little eyes were closing tight in determined efforts to force the sleep that would make the time till morning so much shorter. But in Bethlehem Center were six boys who, it is safe to say, were thinking less of the morrow's gifts than of the morning's plan. For preparations for early rising had been as elaborate as if it were Fourth of July, and there was a solemn agreement that not one present should be looked at until after their return.

Gertrude had fallen asleep, thinking of the letter beneath her pillow that promised her return to college at the beginning of next term. But at the first tinkle of her alarm clock she was up and, dressing by candlelight, went softly down the stairs and out into the keen air of the morning. The stars were still bright overhead, and there was no light in the east. But Gertrude Windsor was not the first abroad, for at the gate Eddie, the two Willies, and little Phil stood waiting, and Harry and Charlie were seen coming at top speed.

"Are we all here?" asked Eddie in a stage whisper, and the other boys huddled close together and wriggled with suppressed excitement.

"Yes," answered Gertrude. "Which place is first?"

"Mr. McKenzie's," announced Charlie, whose part it was to lay out the route.

And crossing the road, they passed through the parsonage gate. Beneath the study windows, Harry, at a given signal, struck the tuning fork against his boot heel. Gertrude gave the key, and then, like one, there rose to greet the dawning of another Christmas day those clear young voices.

"Hark! the herald angels sing,
  'Glory to the new-born King;
  Peace on earth and mercy mild,
  God and sinners reconciled.'"

There were sounds from within before they had finished the first stanza. But when, after the "amen," the pastor started to open the window, the boys were too quick for him. There was a volley of "Merry Christmas," and his answer reached only the rearguard, tumbling over the picket fence.

Beneath the bare apple tree boughs in Harold Thornton's yard, Charlie, Eddie, and little Phil sang "We Three Kings of Orient Are" while the others joined in the chorus. At the song's close the superintendent, swifter of foot than the pastor, overtook them with a great box of candy.

Tears came into the eyes of Mrs. Martin as, watching beside her sick child, she heard again the story of the Babe "away in a manger, no crib for his bed." Old Uncle King forgot for a moment his vexing troubles as he listened to the admonition to "rest beside the weary road and hear the angels sing." Mrs. Fenny cried, as sick people will, when she heard the boys' sweet, triumphant notes.

So from house to house the singers went, pausing at one because of sickness, at another because those within were lonely, at some for love, as they had serenaded the pastor and the superintendent, and bringing to each some new joy.

The stars were fading out, and they had started to return. On their side of the street was the post office, and opposite them was the saloon with its gaudy gilt sign: "Tim's Place." Little Phil was behind Gertrude as they passed that building—it was home to him. His hand just touched her sleeve.

"Do you think—" he whispered, and she could see the pitiful quiver of his chin as he spoke. "Do you suppose . . . we could sing one for m'father?"

Tears filled Gertrude's eyes and, had she not known boys so well, she would have stooped and caught him in her arms. "Why, surely," she answered. "Which one do you think he would like best?"

Phil had shrunk behind her, and beneath the gaze of the other boys his eyes were those of a little hunted animal at bay. "Bethlehem," he said, huskily.

And when Harry had struck the tuning fork, they began to sing together.

> "O little town of Bethlehem,
>   How still we see thee lie!
>   Above thy deep and dreamless sleep
>   The silent stars go by."

The twenty-fourth had been a good day for business in Tim Shartow's place. He had had venison for free lunch; two mandolin and guitar players had been there all the evening; and there was more than $200 in the till. But now, in the quiet of the early morning, as he sat alone, the reaction had come. He remembered how Rob MacFlynn had had too much, and gone home maudlin to the wife who had toiled all day at the wash tub. He thought of the fight Joe Frier and Tom Stacey had had. He did not drink much himself; he despised a drunkard—and these things disgusted him. There was little Phil, too, "the saloon-keeper's boy" . . . and that cut deep. Wouldn't it pay better, in the long run . . .

And then the music floated softly in.

He did not hear the words at first, but he had a good ear. It was the singing that had brought him, as a boy, into the beer gardens. Stepping to the window, he listened, all unseen by those without. There the words reached him:

> "How silently, how silently,
>   The wondrous gift is given!
>   So God imparts to human hearts
>   The blessings of his heaven.
>   No ear may hear his coming,
>   But in this world of sin
>   Where meek souls will receive him."

And until they sang the "amen," Tim Shartow never stirred from the window.

* * *

The storm that had been threatening all day had descended. Without, a blizzard was raging. But within, beside his study fire, the little ones tucked away in bed upstairs, and a book in his hand, the Reverend McKenzie could laugh at weather. A knock at that hour surprised him; but when he saw who stood upon the threshold, he knew how the saloon keeper felt when he posted his bills so many months before.

"Good evening, Mr. Shartow," he said. "Won't you come in?"

The face of his visitor was tense and haggard, for the struggle had lasted the day long. "I've come for help," he answered, shortly. "I guess it's the kind you can give, all right."

For a moment the pastor searched his face. "God bless you!" he exclaimed. "Come in; come in."

And so was wrought again, before the close of the day that had been ushered in by the singing of the carols, the ever new miracle of Christmas. For God's gift to men had been again accepted, and into another heart made meek and ready to receive Him the dear Christ had entered.

Unexpected Christmas

Marguerite Nixon

What can one do when a torrential storm closes off home, and one is forced to spend Christmas Eve with strangers . . . strangers who have so very little . . . just a rather poor farm . . . and some animals in a barn?

This very special Guidepost story has to do with just such a dilemma.

We were well over halfway to our farm in East Texas when the storm broke. Lightning flashed, thunder crashed, and a tree fell with a great ripping noise. When the rain poured in such a flood that we could not see the road, my husband drove off onto what seemed to be a bit of clearing deep in the piney woods.

As we waited I sensed we would not get to the farm that night to celebrate Christmas Eve with our family. We were sitting there, miserable and dejected, when I heard a knocking on my window. A man with a lantern stood there, beckoning us to follow him. My husband and I splashed after him up the path to his house.

A woman with a lamp in her hand stood in the doorway of an old house; a boy of about 12, and a little girl stood beside her. We went in, soaked and dripping, and the family moved aside in order that we might have the warmth of the fire. With the volubility of city people, my husband and I began to talk, explaining our plans. And with the quietness of people who live in the silence of the woods, they listened.

"The bridge on Caney Creek is out. You are welcome to spend the night with us," the man said. And though we told them we thought it was an imposition, especially on Christmas Eve, they insisted. After we had visited a while longer, the man got up and took the Bible from the mantel. "It's our custom to read the story from Saint Luke on Christmas Eve," he said, and without another word he began.

"'And she brought forth her firstborn Son, and wrapped Him in swaddling clothes, and laid Him in a manger.'"

The children sat up eagerly, their eyes bright in anticipation, while their father read on.

"'And there were in the same country shepherds abiding in the field, keeping watch over their flocks by night.'"

I looked at his strong face. He could have been one of them. When he finished reading and closed the Bible, the little children knelt by their chairs. The mother and father were kneeling and, without any conscious will of my own, I found myself joining them. Then I saw my husband, without any embarrassment at all, kneel also.

When we arose, I looked around the room. There were no bright-wrapped packages or cards, only a small, unadorned holly tree on the mantel. Yet the spirit of

Christmas was never more real to me.

The little boy broke the silence. "We always feed the cattle at 12:00 on Christmas Eve. Come with us."

The barn was warm and fragrant with the smell of hay and dried corn. A cow and a horse greeted us, and there was a goat with a tiny, woolly kid that came up to be petted. *This is like the stable where the Baby was born*, I thought. *Here is the manger, and the gentle animals keep watch.*

When we returned to the house, there was an air of festivity and the serving of juice and fruitcake. Later, we bedded down on a mattress made of corn shucks. As I turned into a comfortable position, they rustled under me and sent up a faint fragrance exactly like that in the barn. My heart said, *You are sleeping in the stable like the Christ Child did.* As I drifted into a profound sleep, I knew that the light coming through the old pine shutters was the Star shining on that quiet house.

The family all walked down the path to the car with us the next morning. I was so filled with the Spirit of Christmas they had given me that I could find no words. Suddenly I thought of the gifts in the back seat of our car for our family.

I began to hand them out. My husband's gray woolen socks went to the man. The red sweater I had bought for my sister went to the mother. I gave away two boxes of candy, the white mittens, and the leather gloves while my husband nodded approval.

And when I was breathless from reaching in and out of the car and the family stood there loaded with the gaiety of Christmas packages, the mother spoke for all of them. "We thank you," she said simply. And then she said, "Wait."

114

She hurried up the path to the house and came back with a quilt folded across her arms. It was beautifully handmade; the pattern was the Star of Bethlehem. I looked up at the tall beautiful pines because my throat hurt and I could not speak. It was indeed Christmas.

Every Christmas Eve since then I sleep under that quilt, the Star of Bethlehem, and in memory I visit the stable and smell again the corn shucks, and the meaning of Christmas abides with me once more.

The Red Envelope

Nancy N. Rue

Tom was gone. How could she possibly face Christmas without him? Worse, the children were all acting as if it were Christmas as usual. How could they!

Nancy Rue, of Lebanon, Tennessee, is a frequent contributor to Brio *and* Breakaway *magazines. She is also author of the* Christian Heritage *historical fiction series published by* Focus on the Family. *"The Red Envelope" was the lead story in the December 1997* Focus on the Family *magazine.*

Slice. Scoop. Plop. *I don't feel like doing this.* Slice. Scoop. Plop. *I don't want to do this. I don't want to shop*—slice, scoop, plop—*I don't want to decorate. I just want to skip it*—slice, scoop, plop—*and pretend I didn't notice this year.*

I sliced, scooped, and plopped the last of the dough from the ready-made cookie dough package and shoved the cookie sheet into the oven. They were a far cry from the bejeweled affairs I'd baked for 26 years, and the only reason I'd even summoned up the effort to throw these on a pan was because Ben had opened and reopened the cookie jar four times the previous night before saying, with 14-year-old tact, "What! You're not baking this year? What's up with that?"

He'd gone on to inform me that tomorrow (now today) *was* the twenty-third, and that Ginger and Paul would be arriving in two days, and they were going to "freak" when there wasn't any "cool stuff to eat like usual." This from the same kid who flipped the channel every time a holiday commercial came on and had for years been eschewing all talk of a family photo for the annual Christmas card. I hadn't even considered a family picture this year. A big piece of the family was now missing—or hadn't anybody noticed?

All my friends had been telling me, practically since the day of the funeral, "Michelle, the first year after you lose your husband is the hardest. You have to go through the first Valentine's Day without him, the first birthday, the first anniversary."

They hadn't been kidding. What they hadn't told me was that Christmas was going to surpass all of them in hard-to-take. It wasn't that Ken had loved Christmas that much. He was as bad as Ben and Scrooge put together when it came to holiday advertisements. Said the whole thing was too commercial and that when you really thought about it, Easter was a much more important celebration in the church.

I flopped down on a stool at the kitchen counter and half-heartedly started a list of who I needed to buy for. Ginger had called last night (right after Ben's fourth trip to the empty cookie receptacle), giggling and shushing the dormitory howls behind her.

"I just finished my last final!" she shrieked into the

phone. "I'll be home day after tomorrow. Do you know what I'm looking forward to?"

"Sleeping for 72 straight hours?" I said.

"No." She'd sounded a little deflated. "Seeing all those presents piled up under the tree. I've never cared what was in them or how many were for me; I just like seeing them there. How weird is that?"

Not weird at all, my love, I thought now as I penciled in Ben; Ginger; Paul; his wife, Amy; my grandson, Danny. *Just highly unlikely.*

I hadn't done any shopping. I couldn't even think about my tradition of wrapping every gift so that it was more a work of art on the outside than was the article within. And there had been no way I could spend my usual three days decorating—two hours on the manger scene alone. But my kids were still expecting it, even Paul, who at 25 had a child of his own, and *still* asked me last week when he called if I had the old John Denver Christmas album dusted off yet.

I snapped the pencil down on the counter. None of them seemed to even suspect that this wasn't going to be the usual Tabb family Christmas. They were all acting as if their father's death 11 months ago wasn't going to change a thing about our celebration. As far as I was concerned, there wasn't that much to deck the halls about. Ken was gone. I was empty and unmotivated and, at best, annoyed. At worst, I wished they'd all just open the presents and carve the turkey without me.

When the oven dinged, I piled two dozen plain brown circles on a plate and left a note for Ben: *I don't want to hear any more complaining! Gone shopping. I love you. Mom.*

117

The complaining, however, went on in my head as I elbowed my way through the mob at the mall. *Ken was right*, I thought. *This is all a joke.* It really was everything he hated—canned music droning its false merriment somewhere in the nebulous background, garish signs luring me to buy, squabbling, tired-looking families dragging themselves around, worrying about their credit card limits as they snapped at their children.

Funny, I thought, while gazing sightlessly at a display of jewelry I knew neither Ginger nor Amy would wear, *all the time Ken was here, pointing all this out to me, it never bothered me. Now it's all I can see.*

I abandoned the jewelry idea and took to wandering the mall, hoping for inspiration so Ginger would have something to look at under the tree. It wasn't going to be like years past—I should have told her that. She wasn't going to see the knee-deep collection of exquisitely wrapped treasures that Ken always shook his head over while he grinned at me.

"You've gone hog-wild again," he would always tell me, and then he would add his only contribution. Every year he spent months looking for just the right worthy cause. Instead of buying me a gift, he'd write a check in my name to them, be it the Muscular Dystrophy Association or a local church that needed a new roof, and put it in a red envelope and tuck it onto a branch of our Christmas tree.

"This'll last all year," he'd tell me. "Maybe even change someone's life."

I stopped in mid-mall, causing a pile-up of aggravated shoppers behind me. Ken wasn't there, a fact that didn't seem to bother the rest of my family. But he could still be with me, maybe just a little, if his part of Christmas was.

It wasn't a big spark of Christmas spirit, but it was enough to ram me through Sears and Wal-Mart—and See's candies (Paul liked the cashew turtles). It was also enough to nudge me with the fact that I couldn't put the envelope on the tree if we didn't have a tree. They still had some left at Safeway—and their turkeys looked good too.

The decorations weren't buried too deeply in the garage. I'd barely gotten them put away last year before Ken had his heart attack. I thought about that as I dragged in boxes and untangled lights. The American Heart Association, that was the ticket. I stopped and wrote a check and miraculously located a red envelope in my desk. It would look perfect on this branch. . . . What else to put there? I didn't get candy canes for the tree this year. . . . Maybe I'd string some popcorn.

I was deep into decorating when Ben emerged from the kitchen. "Where are the rest of the cookies?" he asked.

"What do you mean, 'the rest'?" I said. "There are two dozen on that plate."

"Were," Ben corrected.

I rolled my eyes at him as I backed up to check out the tree. "I'll make some more," I said.

"Are you going to put thingies on the next batch?" he said.

When I finished setting up the manger scene, I checked the kitchen for "thingies."

But the next day, Christmas Eve, my spirits sagged again. There is no lonelier feeling than standing in the midst of one's family—a squealing, vivacious college daughter; a sweet, gentle daughter-in-law; a handsome, successful quarter-century-old son; a wide-eyed, super-charged 4-year-old grandson; and even an awkward teenager whose hugs are like wet shoelaces—and being keenly aware that someone is missing. Everyone else seemed to be avoiding the subject.

"The tree is *gorgeous*, Mom," Ginger said. She knelt in front of it and began hauling gifts out of a shopping bag to add to my pile.

"I love what you did with the wrappings, Michelle," Amy said. "You're always so creative."

"I forgot to buy wrapping paper," I told her. "I *had* to use newspaper."

None of *them* had forgotten a thing. There was no sign of mourning—it was Christmas as usual. Ben and Paul sparred over whose stocking was whose, and Danny picked all the M&M's out of the cookies before he ate them, and Ginger picked up every present and shook it. I put on a valiant smile and wished they would all go to bed so we could get this over with.

I stayed up after the last of them and slid my red envelope out from under my desk blotter. The tree lights winked softly at me as I tucked it between a misshapen glittery angel Ginger had made in second grade and Ben's Baby's First Christmas ball.

"I guess they have to go on with their lives, Ken," I whispered. "But I wish you were here."

It occurred to me as I unplugged the lights and groped toward the stairs that they might feel a little ashamed in the morning when they realized what it was. Would there be some oh-yeah-I-remember-he-al-ways-did-that and some gulping and some exchanging of sheepish looks?

I hoped so.

Danny was, of course, up before the paper carrier. I dragged myself into the kitchen and found it already smelling like a Seattle coffee house.

"This is what we drink at school," Ginger told me, and handed me a cup.

"Have they already started on the presents?" I asked.

She shook her head, and for the first time I noticed a twinkle in her eye that was unprecedented for this hour of the morning. "What are you up to?"

"It's not just me," she said.

"Mom!" Paul yelled from the direction of the tree. "Come on! I can only hold this kid off for so long!"

"Come see'm, Grandma!" Danny called. "Come see all these red things!"

"What's he talking about?" I said.

"You'll see," Ginger smiled.

What I saw at first was my family, perched on the couch like a row of deliciously guilty canaries. What I saw next was our Christmas tree, dotted with bright red envelopes.

"Man, it got crowded in here last night," Ben said. "I came down here about 2:00 and freaked Amy out."

"I almost called 911 when I came down," Paul added. "Till I saw it was Ginger, and not some burglar."

I missed most of that. I was standing in front of the tree, touching each one of the five envelopes I hadn't put there.

"Open them, Mom," Ginger said. "This was always the best part of Christmas."

Paul chuckled. "I was afraid everybody had forgotten."

No one had. From Paul, there was a check for Big Brothers, for kids who have to grow up without dads. From Amy, to the church, where she best remembered her father-in-law. From Ginger, for the Committee to Aid Abused Women, "because Dad always treated you like a queen," she said. From Ben, a $20 bill for a local drug program for kids, "since Dad was all freaked out about me staying clean."

The last envelope was lumpy, and it jingled. When I opened it, a handful of change tumbled out.

"That's from me, Grandma," Danny said, little bow-mouth pursed importantly. "For lost dogs—you know, like that one me an' Grandpa rescued."

I shot Paul a question with my eyes.

"He brought it up himself," Paul said.

Amy groaned happily. "He remembered at 5:00 this morning."

I pulled all the envelopes against my chest and hugged them.

"You know what's weird?" Ginger said. "I feel like Daddy's right here with us."

"Yeah, that's pretty weird," Ben said.

"But true," Paul said. "I felt like he's been here this whole time. I thought I'd be all bummed out this Christmas, but I don't need to be."

"Well, Ken," Amy said, holding up her coffee mug. "Here's to you."

Mugs clinked. Laughter danced across the living room.

I began to think about carving that turkey.

His Last Christmas

Joseph Leininger Wheeler

This story evaded me for months. Every time I tried to tackle it, writer's block slammed the door. Perhaps it was because my father's passing was too real to me, and too close—I just could not gain perspective. The deadline for this book came and passed, and still I had no story. Finally, almost in despair when nearly a year had passed, I turned the story over to the good Lord. I took the events, inspired as they were by my father's last few months (even the life story on the wall), and asked Him, if it was His will, to take over my pen. Incredibly, at that very moment, He loosed the logjam in my brain. What you now read, I wrote this afternoon in four hours—without so much as one pause—as March snow lazily fell outside our Colorado gray house.

Thank you, Lord!

Who is he?"

"*He?* Oh, you're new here, aren't you. He's been here for a month or so now. One of the good ones . . . *never* complains; makes up for those who do their best to make our lives a living hell."

"But who *is* he—doesn't he come with a name attached?"

[Laughs.] "Of course he does! Sorry. He's Mr. Abbey."

"*Mister?*"

"Oh, I know it is a bit unusual, calling him 'Mister,' when we refer to most everyone else by first names, but I can't really explain. In time—as you take care of him, talk with him, watch him—you'll know why we call him Mister."

"Now you really have me curious. . . . Is he kind of, you know, old-school formal?"

"Well, yes and no."

"Y-e-s?"

"Let's see, how can I put it? . . . I don't really know myself why it's so, because we have lots of other old men here, and we call 'em all by first name, old school or not. So it's not just his age—it's something more."

"Must be quite a bit more."

"Yes, you could say that. . . . I remember the morning he was admitted. He was wheeled in, and I helped to lift him onto the bed. He is very thin and doesn't weigh much. Has almost no power left with which to move himself. Oh, it's sad! . . . Yet he's not weak inside. Inside, he is probably the strongest person of us all."

"Now you *have* got me intrigued!"

"Is this a good time to talk?"

"Yes, I don't clock in until the afternoon shift. Take as much time as you can spare."

[Leans back in her chair, a far-away look in her eyes.] "Let's see, where was I—Oh, that first morning! . . . No way I can ever forget it. He didn't say much (he doesn't say much). But his *eyes!* His eyes followed me as

121

I moved around the bed and elsewhere in his room. His eyes were friendly—and there was just a smidgeon of a twinkle in them—but they also revealed a reserve I'm not used to in our patients here. They seemed to be weighing me, trying to size me up! That shocked me, because—"

" —most of the others think only of themselves and their problems?"

"You got it! And many of them are darn angry about being here, about being dropped off here by their families, about being defenseless—totally at our mercy—about knowing, deep down, that things will never get any better for them—*that they will die here*."

[A long pause, while she struggles to regain her composure.] "Yes, that's the worst of it. It's a lot like a dialysis wing I worked in a few years ago at Community General. We knew, and they knew, and they knew that we knew, that things were unlikely to get better—or not for long, that is. Almost all of them we'd see died. It broke my heart, so many of them were so young! I finally—finally had to leave. For some dumb reason, I thought it would be different here."

"Well, isn't it?"

"Yes, it is different, but not much. In dialysis, the body is shutting down on them. Occasionally, we'd see a miracle—a new drug, a new procedure, a new diet, healing from within by a higher power than medicine. . . ."

"You believe in God?"

"Yes, I do; no small thanks to Mr. Abbey . . . but that's another story. In dialysis, miracles sometimes happen, and I guess all of us, deep down, hoped a miracle would occur with each of those patients we came to love

the most. But it's worse here: with age, there can be no miracle short of the Second Coming. Once the body begins to dismantle its white blood cell armies, once the inner organs begin to wear out, once the strength begins to ebb away—it's only a matter of time."

"You make it sound depressing. . . . I'm—I'm beginning to wonder if I should have come here."

"Oh, no! I guess I haven't done a very good job of explaining myself. There *is* a difference here—or, rather I should say, there *can* be a difference. There can be a beauty, strange as it may seem, in one's last moments. When one's inner spirit really shows through."

"I think you've lost me."

"All right, see if this helps. Several weeks ago, Charlie, a bone cancer case, was screaming night and day. You literally could not get away from his voice. He was in pain, great pain (every breath hurt), and he made sure every one of his breaths hurt us too—*all* of us! Charlie was angry at life, angry at us, and angry at God. And none of this anger did he keep inside of him—that was not his nature. He was terribly self-centered. His room was next door to 202—Mr. Abbey's room."

"Oh, the poor man!"

"I haven't told you the half of it! Two doors down the hall, on the other side of Mr. Abbey, was another screamer—a woman. She wasn't dying, but, oh, how we wished she would! A fouler-mouthed patient we have never had here. Hour after hour, she would rant and rave, screaming, raging, laughing maniacally. And every other word was a four-letter one."

"And in the middle of this was your Mr. Abbey. How did he take it?"

"Let me tell you. One night I subbed for a friend and took her graveyard shift. Normally, midnight to 8:00 is the quietest of the three shifts, but not *that* night. Both of those patients were virtually out of control. In the midst of it, my nerves on edge and wondering if I could possibly stand one more day of it, I walked in to Mr. Abbey's room to check on him and turn him (he doesn't have enough strength left to even turn over)."

"Oh, how sad!"

"Sad, indeed! Well, he was wide awake (how could he *not* be? Nobody slept that night.). I walked to the head of his bed, and he smiled. I was about to ask him how in the world he could endure it, then I looked into his eyes, and they were filled with concern *for me!*"

"No!"

"Yes, it staggered me. In his quiet and kind voice he said, 'My heart goes out to you and all the others you work with. You are probably wondering *Is it worth it? Could any amount of money possibly compensate for* this?'

"Well, I smiled a rather sickly smile, and said (I had to speak rather loud in order to be heard), 'To tell the truth, Mr. Abbey, the thought *had* crossed my mind.'

"There was a long pause as we both listened to that discordant duet. Then he said, 'I feel sorry for them both.'

"Disbelievingly, I sputtered out, 'For *them?*'

"'Yes,' he answered quietly, '*them*. Mr. Zingfeldt has no faith in God to help carry him through. He can't possibly, judging by what he says—'

"*Screams,* you mean!" I retorted.

"He smiled. 'Yes, *screams* is correct . . . and the other—Mrs. Wilson, is it not?'

"'Yes.'

"'Mrs. Wilson must not believe in God either, or she would not continually take His name in vain.' A look of pain came over his face. 'That is what hurts me deep down inside, every curse against the God I love and serve hurts. More than hurts. Not because I can't handle it, but because she is in such need of the Lord, of a friend. Were I able to move, I'd try to talk with her, offer to be that friend. Same with Mr. Zingfeldt . . .' Then his kind, loving eyes softened, and he said, 'But *you* could be that friend.'

"Almost horrified, I spat out, '*Me?* You've got to be kidding! I'm not sure I still believe in God. And this nightmare we are both forced to endure isn't helping any, that's for sure.'

"There was a long silence, then he said, 'Miss Andrews, would you care to tell me more? This isn't'— and here his eyes twinkled impishly—'a very busy time for me. . . . I have time to listen if you'd care to tell me why you feel as you do.'

"Well, I can't really explain it, but knowing Mr. Abbey had been a minister, I figured *Why not? This night is such a hell; maybe he can bring back some sense to all this—perhaps even to my life itself.* So there by his bedside I told him the story of my life—it has not been a happy one. Several times I broke down and wept. Tears trickled down his face too. My handkerchief did double duty that night. Mr. Abbey was not at all judgmental about the mess I'd made of my life; he just looked at me with his kind and loving eyes.

"It took a long time to tell, and why I'm telling *you* all this, I don't really know; but somehow I feel I can trust you with it."

"Without question. I *promise*. . . . So what happened next? Do you mind telling me the rest of the story?"

"Not at all; might as well finish what I've begun. I spoke to him on and off throughout that awful, yet strangely wonderful, night. Each time I'd complete the rest of my rounds I'd return and we'd talk some more. If ever a person walked side by side with his Lord, surely Mr. Abbey does. Before daylight ended that sleepless night, he brought me back to God—gave me a hope, a reason for living. . . . I've started going back to church."

"I'm—I'm a bit curious. . . . Did you become that friend?"

"Now you put *me* on the spot! Well, yes, I felt I could do no other. I *tried*."

"And failed?"

"Perhaps; yet perhaps not. Mr. Zingfeldt was Jewish and felt that if God would let one-third of his race be snuffed out during Hitler's holocaust, then either that God was not the God the Jewish people have worshiped for thousands of years or, worse, perhaps that perceived God didn't even exist. Believe me, our dialogue got beyond my depth often, and I'd have to get back to Mr. Abbey to seek counsel. It was a strange triad. Then Mr. Zingfeldt entered into his final agony. We gave him powerful drugs because of the excruciating pain. His skin turned blackish and, about a week ago, he died."

"Do you feel you got through?"

"I don't really know for sure. I like to think so. Don't have much to go on, though, for he was so drugged during those last days he lost all sense of reality. But I was with him at the end. Just before he breathed his last rasping, gasping breath, awareness came back into his eyes, and he tried to say something—I never knew what. I reached for his hand, and I felt an answering squeeze (it must have taken his last tiny reserves of strength); he tried to smile . . . and then he was gone."

"And—and the woman?"

"Mrs. Wilson? I had less success with her. She'd just scream at me, curse me—she seemed demon-possessed. Just last Thursday we had her transferred. It was either her or us. So I guess I failed with her."

"Perhaps. Only time will tell."

"Hi there, Janet. It's beginning to look like Christmas."

"It *does*, doesn't it! I was head of the decorating committee this year. First time for me; before, I never felt like it, not knowing for sure if I even believed in Christmas—or Christ. But now I feel differently. I'm filled with so much joy I can hardly contain it."

"I can tell by your laugh. Every time I hear you my day seems brighter—your laugh is *so* infectious."

[Laughs.] "You're kind; others describe it in less flattering terms. . . . But the place does look festive at that."

"And the Christmas carols—is that your idea too?"

"Yes, it seemed like the proverbial horse and carriage—didn't seem right to have one without the other. Oh, by the way, have you been down to Mr. Abbey's room lately?"

"You mean, have I seen the decorated wall everyone's been talking about?"

"That's it! Isn't it something? I understand some of the family put it up. Wasn't easy, as they had to wear masks. So sad about Mr. Abbey's staph infection. He has more company than anyone else in the whole place, and it has made it so much harder for them to talk with him and tell him how much his life has meant to them. . . ."

"That's hard—'has meant.' It won't be long now, will it?"

"No, sorry to say. . . . By the way, Janet, you haven't asked, but I felt if Mr. Abbey could turn *your* life around, well . . . maybe, just maybe, he might be able to salvage *mine*. I didn't see how anyone could possibly mess up more than I have—three divorces and two live-ins."

"Not that I really *needed* to ask. I can tell it by your face."

"You noticed?"

"Couldn't help it."

"Well, yes. Only I was a harder nut to crack than you: it took weeks before Mr. Abbey brought me . . . he brought me . . . to . . . to, uh . . ."

Susan reached for her hand. No words were necessary.

After a long pause, Janet changed the subject. "Back to that wall! As you know, the family put up on it most of the jobs and roles Mr. Abbey has had during his long life. I was so intrigued that I memorized them. Let's see if I can remember them all: salesman, tailor, lumberjack, farmer, teacher, minister, counselor, missionary, administrator (did you know he's even been a college president?), band director (evidently he is an accomplished musician himself, both as a vocalist and with various musical instruments), choir leader, painter, devoted husband and father—oh, the list could go on and on! *Everybody* has been down there to look at it!"

"Kinda sad, isn't it, Janet. Now that we know about his long and successful life we respect him for it. But don't you suppose that *every* patient in this place comes to us with a similar story, if we only knew it? Oh, perhaps not as grand as Mr. Abbey's, but some might come close. In fact, I sometimes wonder . . ."

"Wonder what?"

"Oh, uh, well, I sometimes note how we treat most of our patients. We treat *children* nicer and with more respect than we do them! And I wonder whether or not we would act differently around them if we knew their life stories . . . the way we know Mr. Abbey's."

125

"Hmm. You may have a point there. . . . I'd never thought of it that way. To so many of us, they are not really people at all, but jobs, paychecks, rather unlovely (and often smelly) specimens of not-long-for-this-earth humanity. What a difference it would make if we went to the trouble to really *know* them!"

* * *

"Happy New Year, Susan!"

"Happy New Year to you, Janet."

"Sad, huh?"

"You mean about Mr. Abbey, of course. *Very!*"

"Did—did you get in to see him before Christmas?"

"Of course, but it wasn't easy, with so many others wanting to do the same thing."

"True indeed. I wasn't surprised by the many visitors who came, but I *was* surprised by how many of our coworkers found it necessary to visit that room, surgical mask or not!"

"And did you—did you hear him, uh—"

"—hear him play his harmonica . . . for the last time?"

"No, but I had heard him play before. But I heard it was *so sad*—everyone knew it was the last time. Stephanie told me Bob had to help hold up his harmonica. I'll—I'll never hear a harmonica again without thinking of him."

"Did you look at him?"

"Did I *what?*"

"Did you ever *really* look at him?"

"Oh! I think I know what you are driving at. You mean, his face."

"Yes."

"I did indeed. It was . . . uh, in a way, beautiful. A rather strange word to use, isn't it, in connection with a man's face (especially an *old* man's). But it's true, nevertheless. Strangely enough, several weeks ago the realization hit me that we aren't responsible for our faces when we are young, but we *are* when we get old! Look—intently study—any given face in this entire complex, and you will see truth, reality. . . . Whatever is inside has now seeped through into the face. It can't be hidden, not even by plastic surgery, for no plastic surgeon yet has been able to restore the inner ugliness or evil that can be reflected through one's eyes."

"I hadn't thought of it, but you're right."

"Yes, no matter how handsome or beautiful you were when young, you will be ugly—even repulsive—when old, *unless* you have been beautiful inside."

"True enough! And, on the other hand, even the plainest while young can be beautiful when old."

"Like Mr. Abbey."

"Like Mr. Abbey—not that he was necessarily plain when he was young."

"When did you see him for the last time?"

"Well, not at the very last, for his family was there until the very end. His wife was there a lot—she came to see him as regular as clockwork."

"An old-fashioned romance, they say. . . . Been married more than *60 years!*"

"Yeah, they don't make them to last like that anymore."

"More's the pity."

"No one knew when he would go; we only knew it

would be soon. That last night his daughter, responding to a sixth sense that told her time was running out, made a flying trip to see her father. She took one look at him and knew that *this was it.*"

"We *all* knew. No matter which hall you were in, it was all the same: we didn't speak with mere words—it hurt too much—but if ever eyes mourned the truth, they did that last night.

"I had found an excuse to get down to his room Christmas Eve. The room was full of Christmas cards. The flowers people sent were shared up and down the hall, making it the most festive wing in the place! Several church groups came through the building, singing Christmas carols. (I heard later that each one lingered longest just outside his door.) During one of these I happened to be in his room when he first heard their voices. How his eyes brightened! In fact, the most apt word I can use to describe it is 'radiance.' On his face was a look of radiance not of this earth. He turned to me, and said simply, 'I've always loved Christmas.'

"Curious, I asked, 'Why?'

"He didn't hesitate an instant—he *knew.* 'Because it celebrates the birth of my Jesus on this troubled earth.' It was indeed *his* Jesus: none of us could possibly doubt that Christ was his all in all. . . . But how about *you*—when did you last see him?'

"Oh, it was about the nineteenth or twentieth, if I remember right. Anyway, as usual, I had to come back several times before I caught him alone. It's amazing how many of us sensed he was leaving and wanted a part of him while we still had him."

"Truer words were never spoken!"

"Well, when I came back in for the fourth time, there was in his eyes that look of loving, tender concern for me that always greeted me, only this time it was more intense than ever before, as if he sensed it was our last time together. He smiled, and said, 'This is my last Christmas.'

"I didn't know what to say, for I knew full well he knew that *we* knew it was indeed his last. He took me off the hook. 'I have no regrets, Janet.' (At my specific request he'd finally graduated from 'Ms.' to my first name). 'The Lord has given me a full life, and I am ready to go. And He has given me such a warm and loving family. Actually two of them: my biological children . . . and my children of the spirit, such as you. You are what I find hardest to leave. But it is time. My body'—and here he looked down ruefully to his strengthless arms—'is closing shop on me. Not too long from now my faithful generator will flicker for the last time, and then go out.'

"I could not trust myself to speak.

"'And the next face I see will be that of Jesus!' What joy was in his face and voice! 'And,' he continued, 'in that world without pain, aging, and death, I want to see all my loved ones again. Will you promise to meet me there?'

"Too overcome to even speak, I could only nod mutely. Then George came in, and our last shared moment was over."

Breaking the long silence that followed, Susan said, with trembling lips, "The night he— he— he— left us, I was on duty. We all knew it was coming, coworkers and patients alike. There was an incredible hush. I don't remember a sound except soft footsteps down the hall. I could almost hear the feathered sibilance of angels' wings.

"Then . . . Maria (remember how crusty and sarcastic she used to be?), well, Maria came around the corner, and one look at her face told me everything. *He had gone*.

"I took one look at her tear-stained cheeks and took her into my arms, and I wept. We *all* wept."

* * *

Today life goes on in those halls, but not life ever again as it had been before he came. He came with but one stub of a flickering candle, and left a glow warm enough to light the world.